GROWING UP
Country

LESLIE J. POLLARD SR.

outskirts
press

Outskirts Press, Inc.
http://www.outskirtspress.com

ISBN: 978-1-4787-9165-2

Library of Congress Control Number: 2017912129

Cover Photo © 2018 thinkstockphotos.com. All rights reserved - used with permission.

Outskirts Press and the "OP" logo are trademarks belonging to Outskirts Press, Inc.

PRINTED IN THE UNITED STATES OF AMERICA

ACKNOWLEDGMENTS

Growing up Country is a fictionalized account of events from my family's history. It may be more accurately described as "faction," since the stories are an amalgam of real events and my imagination. While non-fiction requires exactness and corroboration, authors of fiction may use their creativity to transform historical events into stories that adhere only to some level of believability.

Readers who grew up in the South or are familiar with the region will be able to relate to the characters, events, and places in this collection of stories. They will also recognize racial fault lines, family relationships, community activities, chauvinistic attitudes, and other aspects of southern life and culture. *Growing up Country* uses fiction to demonstrate that rural Black people forged their own realities of family, religion, and community. It was not my intention to portray real persons or describe events as they actually occurred. Any resemblance to real individuals living or deceased is purely coincidental.

I am grateful to my family members who provided me with information used as the foundation to develop these stories. I appreciate those who sat for interviews and those who took the time to jot down their recollections of family events. My colleagues at the college where I teach provided suggestions for the narrative and changes in chapter titles that made their way into the final document. I am especially thankful to my students who recommended changes that I used to rewrite story endings and to those who used my framework to restructure some of the characters in a way that was included in the narrative. I am very grateful for their efforts.

Of course, I am responsible for any errors or shortcomings.

Leslie J. Pollard Sr.

TABLE OF CONTENTS

Chapter 1

UP NORTH, DOWN SOUTH

I'd rather be a lamppost in Harlem
than be governor of Georgia.
Negro Folk Saying[1]

*T*oday, Matt Nelms Jr., called Trask, was returning from Rochester, New York to Nelms County, Georgia where he grew up. His parents, younger sisters and brothers, and other relatives still lived in the area. His father, Matt Nelms Sr., had built a new house that Trask had never seen; he was actually born a few miles away in a place the children called "the sticks." His oldest sister Elizabeth, Matt Sr.'s daughter by his first wife Martha, refused to use the nickname "Trask" because she said, "nobody that good to his family ought to be called Trask, too close to trash."

Trask's last trip home was back in the summer of 1955. He had moved "up north" after serving almost four years in the United States army. He was in Korea for two years after being stationed up near Rochester, New York where he moved after his discharge. Trask said that he couldn't live in the South again because there was "too little money and too much hate."

He thought he would be killed, or worse, he would do the killing, if he had to readjust to all the rules White people had for Black folks in the South and, to him, Nelms County was as bad as most places. Matt Sr. thought that race relations in Nelms County were better than other places, but he did not object when Trask wanted to move up North, as he had done when some other children wanted to migrate. He realized the military had changed Trask. Many of Matt's and Rena's grown children – Elizabeth,

Teresa, Catherine, Nellie Mae, and Jay Cee had also moved away up North. Elizabeth lived in Philadelphia, Pennsylvania for almost thirty years before moving back to Nelms County. Many Black folks returned to Georgia and other parts of the South after they thought old Jim Crow had died, though they found his ghost still lingering about.

Family and friends were waiting on Trask to return home on one of his famous visits. Matt Sr. was dressed in his normal attire – a pair of denim overalls over a long-sleeved white shirt, a pair of brogans, and a Stetson crimpled to his satisfaction. In winter, LCDs (long cotton drawers) would have been worn underneath, and for church a matching denim jacket, dress shoes, and a tie might have graced this same oxymoronic outfit. Rena, Matt's second wife, sat on the porch with the newspaper in her hand, wearing her black-rimmed glasses, a long blue dress usually reserved for Sundays, and one of her favorite white sweaters which she wore irrespective of the season. The younger children were also there waiting—the youngest boys, who were twins, Lonnie and Ronnie, as well as Geneva and Rebecca, the children still too young to leave home. Older children, Hattie, Elouise, and Andrew who no longer lived with Matt and Rena were also there.

Some neighbors were there too with their daughters, since Jay Cee, about six years younger than Trask, was coming home with him. Both were bachelors, though Jay Cee was inarguably the ladies' man. Matt's brothers Jake and his son Listervelt (called Velt), and Walton, as well as Rena's only sister, Camille, were there. Some of Matt's employees who worked in his pulp wood business were waiting, including James Willie, Trask's boyhood friend Bobby who grew up "next door," and a couple other young men who were about Trask's age. It was a sizeable group of people gathered simply to greet a hometown boy who had achieved no particular fame. Still, it was not as big a group as the going-away party given for Trask when he left to join the military.

Black people in the country and other parts of the South viewed "up North" in a special way. So did White people, but the perceptions, like most things racial, were miles apart. The White image was conceived in the defense of slavery, forged in the crucible of the Civil War, and enshrined in the myths of the Lost Cause. The Black image was a century in the making and had its origin in the Biblical Promised Land, the destination of escaped slaves hustled to freedom by the Underground Railroad. The Black view was refined by the northern role in the Civil War and emancipation and reinforced by letters, care packages, and money that flowed in from "up nord" after the Great Migration. But nothing sharpened the perception of the North like visits from Black men who came back South wearing stylish clothes, driving nice cars, flashing wallets filled with quick bucks and telling stories of fast women. This image made young Black men restless when they reached what Mama Rena called the "mannish" age. Some people envisioned "up North" as one endless Saturday night where partygoers played out their hedonistic fantasies without interference from White people or the police, a place where men could chase any woman they wished, including a White one, if their interest ran in that direction.

"It must be a good place," they thought, "since the Yankees came down here and freed the slaves."

People sat in chairs or on the ground, or stood around reminiscing about Trask's previous visits and the good times they had. They waited for him to drive up the steep hill to the house driving his grand Cadillac, which dominated most of the conversation. There was no consensus on other topics, but the one thing they all knew for certain was that Trask would be driving a Cadillac. They might have debated aloud about the kind of Cadillac —color, model, year, or even whether it should be called a "Kitty," "Caddy," or "Hog" —but he would be driving a Cadillac, "as sure as God's from Zion."

Over the years, other members of Matt's and Rena's family who lived in Ohio, Pennsylvania, New York, and as far away as California came back home, but their return was nothing like the circus-like atmosphere created by Trask's visits. He didn't come home often, but when he did it was a grand occasion for all to enjoy and cherish the memories for months to come. For one thing, Trask was always loaded with money he had saved for the occasion. He spread money around freely and Rena, in a tone that resembled a child being explained something for the first time, reminded him that money didn't grow on trees. Trask ran an automobile body shop and sold used cars that he rescued from the salt used to clear snow from streets. Salt consumed the bodies of automobiles like predators devouring prey.

But Trask's generosity was legendary on both sides of the Mason-Dixon. It was common knowledge that every ne'er-do-well and supposed friend in Rochester had put "the beg" on him at some time or another. He also drank heavily, and alcohol seemed to have stimulated his beneficent instincts. Rumor had it that when Trask got drunk, a string of "friends" followed him around simply to pick up money that fell from his pockets. But Trask never drank much during his visits home, preferring to spend most of his time smoking cigars, driving around to visit friends in his fancy car, and talking trash.

Younger brother Jay Cee was coming home with Trask. He had followed him to Rochester, where he worked as a painter for General Motors before joining Trask in his paint and body shop business. Cee, as he was called, was said to be the best automobile painter in the state of New York (though no doubt with some exaggeration), but he was always in demand for a paint job. Cee also ran his own pool hall, which was home to some great checker players, many of whom had migrated from the South. Unlike Trask, Cee was a teetotaler who claimed he had a "natural high." He joked that men who drank alcohol admitted to getting drunk enough to kiss a girl on her navel.

"If they got that drunk," Jay Cee joked, "then they got drunker than that." This comment always drew a laugh.

A third brother, Lucius, one of Matt Sr.'s children from a romantic escapade outside matrimony, also lived in Rochester. Lucius, who looked a lot like Matt, also made some famous visits home, but he preferred a *fast* rather than a *fine* car. Since his father didn't own up to Lucius as openly as he did other outside children, he unknowingly tried to date his first cousin Ola Jean. Southern Whites might have practiced that kind of thing at one time, but among Black families, African kinship patterns trumped the emulation of White folks. It didn't really matter though, because Lucius was in love with Lana Jean Wilson, the only daughter of Colonel Rudolph Valentino Wilson, one of Tisdell, Georgia's true-blue veins. The Wilson family did not approve of Lucius; he was light-complexioned, yet not the Wilsons' kind of light, and his hair just didn't make the cut, so to speak; he was uneducated and Lana went to college; and though the Wilsons were not wealthy, they held what they had above those who had less. More importantly, Lucius was illegitimate and deprived of the requisite family connections expected by most of Tisdell's elite.

Once, Lucius and Lana slipped across the Savannah River to a juke joint in a town called McConnell, South Carolina, where the local sheriff stopped them allegedly for a blown taillight. When the sheriff spotted Lana, he pulled out his gun, snatched Lucius from the car, and forced him to lie down on the ground where he threatened to blow his goddamn head off, all of which took place over Lana's vociferous and demonstrative claim that she was a Negro. Despite the absence of any physical evidence, the sheriff finally accepted the possibility that Lana had one drop of Black blood, and ordered the "nigras" to leave his town immediately or run the risk of running into his deputies who were not as open-minded as he was. A few weeks later Lucius, now wearing the newly acquired nickname "Lucky," retrieved Lana from her Tisdell home with the only damn permission he claimed he needed – his own—and headed for New York.

Lucius also owned a used car lot, but he was better known for banking numbers, gambling, drag racing (news of which even reached Nelms County), and pool shooting. Lucky did not work, but he had a full-time job. He was a custodian for Kodak Laboratory, working the night shift with a clean-up crew. Every night Lucius signed in to work and left to go to one of his gaming establishments. When he could not show up, the crew signed the time card for him. These guys did the work, and every two weeks Lucius signed over his pay check to them. After about fifteen years, Lucius had such an impeccable work record that the company tried to promote him. The great irony was that to accept the promotion, Lucius would have had to work days, which he could not do and maintain his businesses. The boss would not allow him to turn the job down or keep his old job, so he quit. The decision must still be a mystery to the managers at Kodak who were deprived of the only employee it ever had who never got sick, never missed a day of work, never complained, was never tardy, never asked for a raise, and *refused* a promotion.

As Trask turned his car off the main road and began pulling up the steep hill slowly toward the house, the nose of the automobile became visible to the twins.

"Dere he," Lonnie yelled. "Dere he."

"Dere he," Ronnie repeated louder than his twin brother, as if Lonnie's announcement was insufficient.

Trask was driving a brand-new 1957 Ford Fairlane 500 four-door hardtop. The car was jet-black, trimmed in gold stripes just above the chrome spears that Trask had meticulously painted on himself. The car had three-inch white wall tires sitting on wire rims that seemed to have been made for one of those European models. It had black-and- red leather upholstery, a tissue dispenser, a record player, and power everything.

Stopping in front of the house, Trask and Jay Cee quickly eased out of the car to greet all the people waiting for them. They stepped out wearing two finely coordinated suits, one blue with gray pinstripes and the other gray with blue pinstripes. The suits, called "rags" in those days, looked like they cost at least $200, which might as well have been a thousand dollars for most Black people in Nelms County. Both wore black Stacy Adams shoes with toes that could have been weapons, but Trask's shoes were spit-shined and he carried a handkerchief that he used to dust them off every few minutes, a habit he picked up in the army. Trask chewed on a long unlit cigar, one of those he said was "special-ordered" from Cuba (special-ordered because Trask's buddy Zimmie was from Pocono Beach, Florida, and took orders for cigars whenever he went home because he could buy them cheaper there than in New York).

All gathered around to greet Trask and Cee, who were shaking hands and hugging people like two politicians running for an important office—except that there were no Black politicians in Nelms County and White politicians did not worry much about the Black vote until one of them showed up at a Black church at election time.

"Hi, Mama," Trask greeted Rena after making his way through the crowd to the porch where she sat.

Rena loved that porch, though its only view was the trees beyond the driveway, and sat there many hours, probably pondering the many ways of the world. Even at night, she sat on the porch waiting for Matt and the kids to come in from the grocery store down across the road. When Trask greeted his mother, he slipped a wad of cash into her hand, which he had obviously put together before he arrived. Rena did not smile much—everybody agreed that Rena was not a smiler—but as she took the money and stuck it securely down in the pocket of her sweater, she managed a quick grin without parting her lips, like someone stood behind her with a string pulling her lips in opposite directions.

The twins Lonnie and Ronnie, now about twelve years old, each received a crisp five-dollar bill, after which they quickly ran into the house and hid it in their room, not having any pockets that could be trusted with their good fortune. Returning from the house, the "doubles," as some people called them, without notice found their way inside the 1957 Ford. In his haste to greet people, Trask had left the key in the ignition. The boys began tugging and pulling at things in the car and somehow switched the car on and started raising and lowering the electric windows and the antenna. Before long they had slammed the doors, turned on the radio, pushed in the cigar lighter, pulled tissue from the chrome dispenser and toyed with the record player, the likes of which they had never seen. Soon, one of the boys knocked the car out of gear and it started rolling slowly toward the big hill where the old house sat.

"There go de car!" Uncle Jake yelled. "Somebody better do something!"

Before long, Lonnie and Ronnie were screaming for their lives as Jay Cee ran and overtook the car at the top of the hill. He opened the door as he ran, jumped in the car, put on the emergency brakes and pushed hard on the brake pedal. With the car halfway down the hill, Jay Cee managed to start the engine, thus empowering the brake booster, making it easier to stop. Cee drove the car back up the hill and parked it, carefully putting on the parking brake and removing the keys and handing them to Trask. Cee saved the day, to say nothing of the boys' lives, though the car probably posed more threat to Matt's store across the road than to the boys. One at a time, Trask snatched the twins out of the car by their ears.

The incident now brought everybody's attention to Trask's new car, an occurrence that he had looked forward to. Two years earlier the crowd's attention focused almost immediately on his 1953 Cadillac. They recalled that the Cadillac, or "Kitty" as most called it, had four doors with door handles surrounded by chrome guards, shiny window vents overhead, chrome around the edges of the doors, and one of those visors over the windshield that made the car look like it was wearing a cap. It was black with a white top with what looked like ten coats of paint, and wide white wall tires. The interior was black-and-white leather that matched the outside finish.

The men and women now gathered around to look at this new black Ford, which brought a huge smile to Trask's face. Trask had ordered the car with all the options and insisted on driving it from the showroom floor. He wanted a "virgin," his word, that he could break in himself, rather than one that had been driven by test drivers.

"Trask, where de Caddy?" Bobby asked, interrupting the grin on Trask's face and startling him with the question. "Dat Cadillac you had before had a fine finish wid dem clean lines, and moun-tains of chrome. What you do with the Kitty, Trask?" Bobby continued.

To Black folk, a Cadillac was not just an automobile; it was an occurrence, a concept, a symbol of the Black man overcom-ing all the obstacles the White man had put in front of him. The Cadillac epitomized the motivation behind the great migration from South to North, the material incarnation of all it meant to move to the promised land. As certain as the stalks of cotton in Matt's field symbolized southern toil, the Cadillac evoked escape to a better life.

"I traded the Cadillac two weeks ago," Trask said, a little dis-turbed by the question. "I ordered this baby from the manufac-turer with no miles on it." This statement seemed to land on deaf ears.

"Trask with no Cadillac; I thought I would never see the day.

Things must be awfully slow 'up nord" these days," Uncle Jake claimed.

"No Hog, huh Trask, your bizness must be really founderin' dese days," old man Wilson, a neighbor chimed in.

"Founderin'? What's that? My business fine," Trask said as he became more irritated by the turn of events. *Don't these people see that this is a brand-new car?* "That's a damn…" Trask caught himself. "That's a brand-new 1957 Ford, a 500, top of the line. My Cadillac was two years old, TWO YEARS OLD when I was here last. That's a brand-new car, zero miles when I bought it," Trask repeated more emphatically, but nobody seemed to be listening.

"Dat Cadillac was somem' else; this here a Ford, F - O - R -D – Found On Road Dead," Jake said laughingly.

"I thought it was F - O - R - D, Fix Or Repair Daily," another laughed.

"Trask, looks to me like you done gone from sugar to shit," James Willie claimed, as others agreed.

"Ya'll leave muh boy alone," Matt said. "This is a fine car, you all just jealous 'cause you ain't got no car at all."

"Yeah, Matt you sure right, but this 500 looks like a 100 compared to that Cadillac," Walton said.

The men started walking down the hill toward Matt's store, leaving the women and small children behind as manly talk was now about to take place. Lonnie, Ronnie, and other adolescent boys tagged along with the men to listen as a kind of rite of passage. Conversations would now cover a wide range of topics dominated by southern racism, that is, how White people were more hateful "down South" than "up North."

As they walked together they shook their heads in disbelief that Trask actually drove a Ford. Trask reluctantly joined in the talk, but deep down inside he felt hurt, deprived of that special moment Blacks cherished when they returned from "up North" to bask in the glow of success among family and friends. Jay Cee had warned Trask before they left Rochester not to expect much to be made of this Ford.

No wonder my little brothers had to almost kill themselves just to get them to notice the damn thing, Trask thought.

At this moment, he longed for a Cadillac and swore he would never come south again in anything but a Cadillac.

By the time the group arrived at Matt's store the talk had turned to tales, many of them they had heard numerous times.

"Matt you know what the young bull said to the old bull? Why don't we run down that steep hill and screw about half them heifers?" Walt said.

"And what did the old bull say?" Matt asked.

"The old bull said, I got a better idea; why don't we *walk* down that steep hill and screw them *all*." A hearty laugh followed.

Significantly, old age was still respected in the country and the bull, a symbol of male virility, held a special place in the culture.

It was Cee who shared the funniest joke of the night when he told everybody about this "Negro" he once saw in a bar in New York City. He said that the man moved to Harlem straight from the Mississippi Delta and after settling in with one of his cousins, he went into this neighborhood bar called "Silk and Suds," carrying a bag and a .22- caliber pistol. He put the bag and the gun on the counter and ordered a shot of whiskey.

"Look man, I run a decent place here I don't want no trouble," the bartender said while signaling the waitress to call the police.

"I don't mean no harm, just want a glass of liquor like everybody else," the newcomer said.

The bartender poured some liquor into a glass and handed it to the man. After taking a large drink and wiping his mouth on his shirtsleeve, the migrant took the pistol from the counter and shot into the bag. Some customers ducked for cover, but most ran out of the place, fearing for their lives. About two minutes later the man again took a large drink of liquor and again shot into the bag. The police arrived shortly thereafter. One of them took the man's gun and opened the bag to find a large portion of what looked like cow manure, causing the policeman to grab his nose and drop the bag.

"What is this shit doing in this bag?" the officer asked.

"I heard that all Negroes did it 'up North,'" the migrant explained to the policeman.

"Did what?" the officer asked.

"I heard that the only thing they do up North is drink liquor and shoot the shit." Loud laughter followed.

When the tale-telling ended a checker game started with a different kind of trash-talking. Matt Sr. reigned as checker champion, followed by Cee and brother Kalem who lived across the street, and up to this point had not taken part in any of the festivities. Trask didn't play checkers as well as his brothers, and tonight he couldn't even beat the chumps, too absorbed in thinking how foolish he was to come home in a car other than a Cadillac.

Chapter 2

THE OLE BABY MAKER

My old man's a white old man,
And my old mother's black,
My old man died in a fine big house,
My ma died in a shack.

Langston Hughes[2]

*I*n late July, 1895 Maelue Nelms decided it was no longer possible to hide her pregnancy from her mother Edna. She would never have thought to tell her father Preston without first getting her mother's support, but her mother was not sympathetic. As a devoutly Christian woman, Edna threatened to put Maelue out of the house for getting pregnant without a husband and bringing disrespect upon the family. For a couple of years now Maelue, a high-yella girl of sixteen, had fancied herself a woman and her mother had said many times that she was too "omlish" for her own good. An unwed mother was bad enough, but Maelue's pregnancy was a double dose of trouble, having been impregnated by some no-good Irishman named Michael McCree. Worse still, Maelue refused to say McCree had taken advantage of her—which if he had, might have saved the family's reputation, but she was unwilling to say that which was not true. She had also deprived her father of his patriarchal duty of forcing a shotgun wedding by lying in disgrace with a White man. Maelue had defiled herself not only in the face of her family, but also the church, which was certain to put her out; Rev. Denison didn't tolerate unwed mothers in Rosemont Baptist Church.

With no reason to doubt her mother's word, and having to

face the wrath of her father alone, Maelue ran away from home. Nobody claimed to know where she went for several days, but if the truth be told, the family always understood she was at her paternal grandmother's house. Cora Nelms, called "Murrh" by most people, was also a Christian, but of the practical variety where compassion overruled precept. "Let those without sin …" she would say, rarely completing the verse. Grandmother Nelms and Papa Ed took Maelue and her soon-to-be child into their home, a small house with only modest furnishings. They had very little in the way of worldly possessions, but if you ever heard Murrh laugh, you could tell that her spirit was bountiful. Besides, everyone knows that Black grandmothers always have room for a deserted daughter, a good-for-nothing son, a forsaken child, an abused wife, even a needy neighbor. Their generosity is as broad as Christian charity and unrestrained by material possessions.

When Maelue's child was born on December 5, 1895 he was as White as any baby born to the other Nelms family several miles down the road near Drayton, the county seat. Murrh, with Maelue's consent, named the child Matt Nelms and cared for him like her own. The McCree name was not considered, for obvious reasons, and for the fact that he was what White people called a "po cracker," a term rarely used among Black people.

The White Nelms family had given its name to Nelms County when it was established in 1848 as the twenty-ninth county of Georgia. After the Civil War, the county lost much of its acreage to Horne County, which was carved from it and named in honor of a local Confederate soldier who had served heroically under the command of General Robert E. Lee, Commander of the Confederate forces. The Nelms county seat was Drayton, located in the central part of the county. It had only about 100 people as late as 1950, so the largest city was more than twenty miles away at Tisdell in Oglethorpe County, one of the oldest counties in the state. It must have had twenty thousand people in 1950, perhaps half of whom were Black. Tisdell was a textile town, and those Blacks who were not in the fields or doing domestic work found jobs at the mills. The Savannah River flowed up through all three counties and played a major role in their economies.

Black people had lived in this area as long as anyone could remember. Way back in the middle of the 18th century, the Nelms family owned slaves even when it was outlawed in Georgia. It wasn't illegal, because Georgians were some kind of nascent abolitionists; old man Stewart Nelms' great-grandfather smuggled slaves in from South Carolina. At one time, the Nelms family was the largest slaveholder and owned much of the land in the county. Their slaves counted themselves lucky to belong to "good" White folks, and after emancipation many of the Black Nelms stayed on as tenants and sharecroppers. The patriarch of the family, Stewart Nelms, had prided himself on never having to whip a slave. Some say he had Quaker in his background, which accounted for this reputation.

Matt grew up rapidly and had much curiosity about things. Everyone said he had a good head on his shoulders and was going to be a good businessman someday. There wasn't much chance for schooling in the country when Matt was growing up, but the county started about ten elementary schools (first through seventh grade), in one-room frame buildings in each community, usually named for the neighboring Black church. A higher grade was added each year beginning in the 1940s, and a real high school was constructed in 1955. Matt learned to read and write well despite little formal schooling, because of his grandmother's teaching. He liked reading about farming in the almanacs and learned to draw pretty pictures of flowers, houses, and animals that family members kept for years. His penmanship was very fancy and he had a good acumen for numbers.

When Matt was a teenager, he wrote letters for Grandma Nelms to different people, mostly people he understood to be relatives. Grandma Nelms could write well, but she thought Matt needed the practice to improve his penmanship and spelling. On several occasions, he wrote letters to a man named Stewart Nelms (he is dead now and the family business is headed by his grandson Stewart Nelms III, who is called "Buddy"). Matt didn't know who he was at the time, and Grandma rejected his questions about him.

"For me to know and you to find out," was her reply.

The letters requested shoes, clothing, help of some kind, and sometimes money. Soon afterwards, a big package would arrive by mail, or a Black man would show up driving a big car carrying a large box. He didn't generally say much, but nodded his head a lot. It was many years before Matt connected his Grandma's letters to those packages. Evidently there was some understanding between her and old man Stewart Nelms that she would ask him for things and he would give them to her. Some old folks claimed it was rather commonplace in the South for wealthy White gentlemen to arrange to help their bastard children who were deprived of their rightful inheritance. Evidently Matt's father was not that kind of gentleman, since no letters were ever written to him.

The summers in Nelms County were hot and humid and virtually everything slowed down from June through September. It was during the record hot summer of 1917 that Matt, now a twenty-two-year-old who worked the family farm, was introduced to Martha Hester, whose family had recently moved to the area. They met one Saturday afternoon when Matt and some friends went to Lamb's pond, the only place other than the creek where Black people regularly went to fish, swim, and hang out. The Lambs were a wealthy White family that employed Blacks on their farm and in their dairy, and befriended them by making loans and intervening with the authorities. On this Saturday, Martha and her older sister Ethel had gone to the pond for the first time. Matt and Martha fell in love, and after a brief courtship they married and rented a little house a half mile from the Nelms family farm. The next year Martha gave birth to a little girl named Elizabeth, who was delivered by the midwife "Miss Hilda."

They were happy together, Matt and Martha, but when the influenza epidemic came in 1918, Matt lost Martha to the disease. It was said that the Spanish Flu killed millions of people all over the world, and in the United States more people died than were killed in the Civil War. Hundreds of people in Nelms County came down with the flu, almost every family had some sick; some lost two or three members. For several months Rosemont had services seemed like every few days, they had such a time burying the dead. In the city of Tisdell, there were so many sick people that the schools were converted into infirmaries. Matt himself came down with the disease while in the city doing business. Many thought he was dead, since nobody knew where he was for several days. Because he got sick in the city where his racial identity was not well known, Matt ended up on the White side of the Tisdell Hospital; his later being identified as a Nelms provided no reason to reverse the decision. Matt claimed that his color saved his life, but since so many Whites died in that hospital, another explanation is more plausible. He remembered thinking that he had Martha's child to take care of and thereafter when he got sick he would dream of his youngest child and get up the next day fully recovered. At least that's what he said in later years.

The midwife and neighborhood "doctor" Mrs. Hilda Grayson, better known as Miss Hilda, said that she had never seen anything like this 1918-1919 flu epidemic. That didn't stop her from concocting a treatment, as she did for every other illness, called a "tallman" (perhaps meaning talisman) to keep her clients from catching the disease. She said those who contracted the flu were attacked from inside by a demon that caused blood to ooze from noses, mouths, ears, and anuses – not Miss Hilda's word. Old people said her remedy was no more than some garlic, salt, quinine, and sassafras. Those other ingredients notwithstanding, her "patients" counted on the garlic to ward off the alleged demon. Miss Hilda also claimed the flu made White folks black—that's why they buried them so quickly—but provided no evidence to corroborate the point. Miss Hilda passed her skills on to her spinster daughter, Miss Pleutsy, who continued midwifery and doctoring after her mother died.

After Martha's death, Elizabeth was primarily cared for by Matt's mother Maelue, who had married Gordon Johnson some years earlier. Matt, his stepfather, and his grandparents worked the farm land cooperatively for about four years before Matt remarried. In the fall of 1923, Matt was driving his truck down Ramsey Road a few miles from Drayton when he saw a young girl named Rena Staten with her two brothers, Bertha (Bert) and Nathaniel (Nate). Matt knew Bert rather well and had met Nate, but had never seen their sister. He stopped to speak to the brothers, who introduced him to Rena, who at the time was only fourteen years old—half Matt's age! She wore no makeup and dressed plainly, but Matt thought Rena was very pretty. She was dark-complexioned, a stark contrast to Matt's white appearance, with a keen nose and lips, features Tisdell's bluebloods would have considered a source of redemption.

Matt was so taken with the beautiful Rena he spent the night tossing and turning like a boat in a storm. Every day he saw her face everywhere he went, and with each new sighting he became more determined to court her. A week later he went back to Ramsey Road where she lived, hoping to run into her or even her brothers. He saw Nate going down the road with a bucket. He knew Bertha better than he did Nate, but decided to talk to him anyway.

"Hi, Nate," Matt said.

"How you? You Matt, ain't you?" Nate asked, even though he knew full well who he was, since he had been present when Matt talked to his brother Bertha.

"That's right. Where is Bertha today?" Matt queried.

"Bert working in the field. Um going to the spring," Nate said matter-of-factly. He wondered why Matt was holding this conversation with him. Why this sudden interest? he wondered.

"How old did you say your sister Rena was, Nate?" Matt finally got around to the point of his conversation.

"Didn't say how old she be, but she a lil young fer your old ass, if dat's what you gittin at," Nate said, a little annoyed after he realized why Matt had taken an unexpected interest in him.

"Well, gotta go. See you, Nate," Matt said after a moment of reflection.

Matt realized that he wasn't going to get much encouragement from Nate. That's why he wanted to see Bertha. He decided Bertha had a lot more sense than this stupid brother Nate. After a few more days agonizing over Rena, Matt remembered something his grandma always said:

"If you got to fight the bull, you got to tackle him by the horns." If you have a problem, face it head on and stop going at in a roundabout way. The next day he made his mind up: come hell or high water, he was going to see Rena. He was going to grab the bull by the horns. He drove right up to the Statens' house and knocked on the door. When Mrs. Eunice Staten answered, he introduced himself as Matt Nelms, hedged a little by claiming to be her son Bertha's very good friend, and without further conversation asked for permission to court her daughter Rena.

Matt was unprepared for such an unfriendly response, but perhaps he should have been. He was twice Rena's age, had been married, and had a child by his late wife Martha, and by this time had two outside children by women whom he chose not to marry. His reputation had long preceded him to the Staten household, so he got three swift and forthright answers to his question.

"No, hell no, and get your ass out of my house, you ole baby maker," Eunice Staten said with a mouthful to follow. "Rena is too young for you, so go marry one of the mothers of your illegitimate children. Nothing good can come of you seeing my child; get out, you ole baby maker."

Mother Staten had tagged Matt with an indelible label. These words gave Matt the impression that his visit was anticipated. Why else would she say the same thing as Nate unless stupid Nate had mentioned their conversation to her? It is not clear whether arrogance or chauvinism kept Matt from realizing that Mrs. Staten's reaction was understandable due to his own irresponsible behavior.

Yet none of this deterred Matt, who could not get over Rena. He finally got a chance to talk to Bertha, who said that Rena had been asking about him too since their mother had run him off. Rena had suitors—that is, boys who showed an interest—but none caught her eye quite like Matt, despite his reputation (one cannot assume that Rena liked him because of his reputation). Matt saw Rena at her church, where he went several times, but mostly with Bertha's help, they met secretly. Mama Staten's understandable but hard-core position had pushed a desire for an open courtship into an underground relationship. After a few months, they concocted a plot to marry, with Bertha's help.

One Saturday, while Mother Staten was getting ready for her "ciety" meeting at Friendship Missionary Baptist Church—or "the Mountain," as most people called it— Bertha told her that he was going fishing and Rena was going along. This wasn't unusual, since Rena often tagged along with the boys. While mother Staten was dressing, Rena packed her few things in a small suitcase and slipped them into Bertha's room. They left the house and walked down to Ramsey Road, where Matt met them in his truck and drove to Drayton, where they were married by a justice of the peace. A month earlier, the blood test and marriage license had been acquired by the same general plan.

When Mother Staten learned about the marriage, she was so furious that Bertha had to stay with a relative for weeks before he could come home, and even then it wasn't pleasant for him. For months Mrs. Staten could not stop mumbling to herself, "that old baby maker! With my child, Lord, have mercy, she's go have all them children. Lord, please help my child—that ole baby maker."

Matt's new family now included Rena and Elizabeth, who returned to live with her father and his new wife in a house out in nowhere land. It had plenty of farmland, and Matt saw each acre as a source of hope for the future. In 1926, after two years of marriage, Trask (Matt Jr.) was born and every two years thereafter another child followed until there were thirteen, eight girls and five boys, with one set of twins, Lonnie and Ronnie.

Grandmother Staten never ceased to call Matt "the old baby maker," now with more evidence than she ever wished for, but in time she warmed up to her son-in-law for two reasons. First, his light complexion helped fuel the rumor that the Staten family had an unspoken goal to lighten up the family, even though no one accused them of some deep-seated self-hatred. To the Statens. the goal was a practical matter, like learning to read or cipher, to expand economic opportunity. To others, it was a curiosity why one of the best-looking families in the county wished to spoil such beauty with whiteness. Nevertheless, dark-skinned people fought back with the response "the blacker the berry the sweeter the juice" and the claim that dark skin aged slower than light skin, or as they put it, "black don't crack." They particularly resented the backhanded compliment "black but beautiful" because they found the "but" inherently insulting.

It was the second reason that mattered most to Eunice Staten. Despite his shortcomings, Matt Nelms was a hard-working, ambitious man who cared deeply for his family. He always ran a farm and started selling produce from his truck and house, and over the years operated three grocery stores. He ventured into other businesses that included running a saw mill, raising and curing tobacco, and by the 1950s, operating a pulp wood business, though none matched his success as a grocer. He was respected by Blacks and Whites and enjoyed a good credit rating among business men, especially at stores owned by Jews in Tisdell.

Even Matt's "baby making" had a goal. He wanted to father many sons so he could be a big-time farmer like White men, raising many bales of cotton and helping his sons follow in his footsteps. He advocated cooperating with Whites and starting a business which would insulate them from the worst features of segregation. Unfortunately, the boll weevil ravaged cotton crops, and nature (at one time he had four girls in a row that he called his "stair steps") and migration (many of his children left for the North) ended his dream of a mega farm.

Chapter 3

GROWING UP COUUNTRY

A fine cradle will not always ensure
a fine character.

African Proverb[3]

C hildren who grew up country didn't think of themselves as poor, since virtually everybody was in the same boat, so to speak, and one's worth was more determined by character than material possessions. The Nelms children had a little more stuff than most families, and some of them even thought they were rich. Other people believed so too, since they were always borrowing things – a cup of this, a cup of that. With a father engaged in his own business and a mother who didn't work for White folks, children had some right to this line of thinking. Whatever was missing in their lives, they didn't know about it and when they were older and realized they were not materially wealthy, they considered themselves rich in spirit.

Matt and Rena were protective and loving parents who believed money was no substitute for such values as honesty and hard work. They set the example by rising early every morning and working all day. They were also strict disciplinarians, but their bark was worse than their bite. The one infraction not subject to mitigation was lying. You could get away with most anything else, like skipping chores or slipping away to the creek, but if caught lying you paid a prime price. Of course, the children didn't buy into their parents' claim that their punishment was really more painful to them.

Rena was a quiet, unemotional type who used words like they

were some kind of consumable item like sugar or salt. When Rena rose in the morning, she got fully dressed, and the children had to do the same thing even when there was no school. She dressed in clothes that made her look older than her years, perhaps because she married a man twice her age. Unlike many women in the country, she did not wear hats and never tied her hair in a rag because it reminded her of slavery. She liked wearing a scarf and loved sweaters, as long as they weren't red. She insisted that she was too dark to wear red even though other Black women thought it was an insult to tell them they couldn't wear red. Rena didn't swear, drink or use snuff. Her only vice was a love for coffee, sans cream, despite her insistence that coffee made you black. The cup had to be filled all the way to the brim, set in a saucer to catch the overflow, and piping hot so that it had to be sipped. While most of the family preferred Maxwell House, Rena drank only one brand, Nescafé, or as she called it "Nas-Café." When she said it she held the "nas" – n-a-a-a-s - while letting go of the café – n-a-a-a-s café. To Rena it was Nescafé and not Maxwell House that was good to the last drop.

Like most children growing up country, the Nelms children had grandparents and great-grandparents who played a vital part in their lives. Rena's mother was called Ga-ma by the children, but her friends called her "Snow." While she did everything in a hurry, Matt's grandmother, Murrh, was a slow-motion type – she walked slowly, talked slowly, and was slow to condemn. The most memorable thing that they had in common was a fondness for a sip of whiskey and a dip of snuff. Murrh was hard to get along with when she didn't have snuff under her bottom lip and seemed really to be in pain. When Elizabeth was a little girl, she used to steal a pinch or two out of her cup every now and then and hide it in a jar in the closet. When Murrh was without it, Elizabeth delighted so in giving her what she had hidden for a rainy day.

Both Ga-ma and Murrh had treatments for illnesses that

had been handed down for generations. Store-bought items like three-sixes and castor oil were bad enough, but their concoctions were intolerable. Cow's fat, sassafras tea, and lemon with a little whiskey for colds wasn't so bad, but gargling boiled chinaberries left a rotten taste in your mouth. Rabbit tobacco was used to treat several ailments, and the leaves of other plants were laid across the forehead for fevers and used for infections. Chewing tobacco or a little cornmeal was applied to a hurting tooth, and cuts got some spider web, a touch of snuff, or mud from a "dirt dobbler's" nest to seal the wound. Some burns were treated with a spread of lard, and insect bites got fat and a penny. The success of these remedies may be in doubt, but they were the first line of defense for those who grew up country.

When a little high school was all one needed to teach, Ga-ma Staten taught school near Vidalia, Georgia which she says was below the "gnat-line." Perhaps teaching was the source of her nuggets of wisdom. When she was certain of something, she said "as sure as God's from Zion" – at least that's what the children thought for a long time, but it turns out she was saying "as sure as gun's iron." Another of her adages, "an even swap ain't no swindle," became Matt's business philosophy. Her lack of tolerance for disobedience was explained in the following: "You get nothing out the children you don't put in the raising."

This was her version of several scriptures found in Proverbs, including her corollary: "A hard head totes a sore ass." This was her take on the passage that read "spare the rod and spoil the child." In Ga-ma's case a branchless limb, called a switch, from a nearby tree was the instrument of choice.

As you can see, Ga-ma Staten sometimes had a nasty mouth not just from snuff. When "pooting" and "passing gas" would do for everyone else, she called it "farting." When someone broke gas out loud mother Staten was the only one who didn't flee.

"Don't have to run from the loud ones because they jump

over the turd; it's the quiet ones that come through the turd that you should run from, but you don't know that until it's too late," she explained.

Perhaps the worst thing Ga-ma said was the time she caught her granddaughter Nellie Mae lip-locked with a boy named Buster. She pulled her aside and whispered:

"Girl, don't you know kissing is as close to screwing as farting is to shitting."

The first house Matt and Rena lived in was out in nowhere land, the older children called it "the sticks," but Matt had plenty of farm land, and to him each acre was a source of hope for the future. The house had two bedrooms, a small sitting room, a kitchen, and a little added room outside with a separate entrance. The furnishings included two beds with cotton mattresses, a bureau, a trunk, and a sofa. A picture of Booker T. Washington hung on the wall of the sitting room that had been plastered with newspapers using house paste. The only books were a Bible, a hymnal, and an almanac. Every night Matt read the Bible, sang a hymn, and kneeled by the bed post, sometimes with a child in his arms, and prayed. After he became a deacon, the Bible and hymnal accompanied him to Sunday service and Wednesday prayers. Matt prospered living in "the sticks," despite the nation's depression. When most people in 1935 didn't have a car, he owned a 1933 Ford, and the next year he traded it on a '35 Ford.

About fifty feet away from the house was the family's outhouse, where newspapers doubled as wall and toilet paper (a corn cob or leaf occasionally served the latter purpose). An outhouse was about a four-foot-square structure built out of old lumber and unpainted. Most of them had a single, round, wooden seat, but the Nelms' outhouse was a double, though no one shared it with anyone. To ensure privacy, outhouses didn't have windows, just a front door with a latch inside and a flat, slant back roof that leaked when it rained. Many pondered when doing their business how the rain managed to get in while the smell seemed permanently imprisoned. The back bottom portion of the outhouse was open, and sometimes snakes found their way inside, which made them unsafe at night, so slop jars were used in the bedrooms. Those brave enough to risk using an outhouse at night took a candle to see. One night one of the girls set the candle down near some newspapers that caught her gown on fire and she barely got out alive, but the old outhouse didn't make it.

Around 1936-37 things began to go badly on the agricultural side of the farm and Matt raised more cows and hogs and vegetables to sell. It was these bad times that gave Matt the notion that he might be able to get away with making a little moonshine, and he almost went to jail. Matt saw the sheriff coming and ran into a tree, but the sheriff let him off with a fine. He traded his '35 Ford for a saw mill and bought a truck. The saw mill was short lived, but the children were fascinated to see the saw slicing the bark off the trees and then sawing them uniformly into lumber. When the mill failed to make the kind of money Matt desired, he concentrated on buying and selling more farm animals. A running joke was that if Matt went to the stockyard and bought a ten-dollar cow and someone offered him eleven dollars on the way home, Matt took him off the truck.

By the end of the 1930s, Matt began to prosper again and the family moved into a plantation house he rented from the Lamb family. Everybody called it the BIG HOUSE. It was near the fork of the roads that led to Tisdell and Drayton. The house didn't face either road, but faced the fork where the roads diverged. It was two stories with worn white paint and pine floors. The house had eight large bedrooms — four downstairs and four upstairs – all with fireplaces. The family rarely used the upstairs except to store things and when a visitor came; it was that big. It had long hallways both downstairs and upstairs and closets the size of the rooms in "the sticks." There was a beautiful staircase with ivory rails on the side where the children would slide down them. It had a porch that wrapped all the way around the house like a belt. The Lambs also left beautiful furniture, including a leather sofa and chairs. The house was like a mansion and the children later said it was like something from *Gone with the Wind*.

Outside there were large oaks, forsythia, and shrubs with tiny white flowers (but nobody knew their name), and crepe myrtles grew alongside the road. There were beautiful dogwoods whose branches were used to make brooms – there was no grass. Matt also took small dogwood twigs about three to five inches and hit one end with a hammer to flare them into bristles that everyone used as toothbrushes. There were rock formations in the front that were once flower beds. Across the road was the coldest, deepest well in the county. The water was always very clear and clean until a dog fell in before it was covered for protection. He was fished out, but not before he died; after that the family was not so proud of that well. There was also a scary attic because Matt told the kids ghosts lived up there to keep them out. Periodically, someone from the Lamb family would come and explore the attic for antiques. One time, one of those Lambs showed up to rummage through the attic and brought a dead rattlesnake with him that he said he had killed in the road. He skinned the thing right there on the porch and said he was going to make himself a belt.

The Big House was a special place. All around the place were pear trees, pecan trees, crabapples, fig trees, and wild plums with blackberries and gooseberries in the nearby woods. From all these the family made preserves and pies that the children loved. There were cows, pigs, chickens, goats, turkeys, and guineas. The garden had melons and all kinds of vegetables that Rena and the girls prepared every day. Potatoes were cooked in the fireplaces where ash cakes were made, even though people spat in the fireplace, particularly those who used tobacco or snuff. The cows produced plenty of milk, which was good (to make butter) except when the cows ate wild onions that sprang up here and there in the pasture. Once in a while, Matt and the boys went fishing and hunting and killed mostly quail, rabbits, squirrels, and occasionally brought back a "possum" or coon, which was cooked in a big pot with potatoes. Corn, butterbeans, and other vegetables were planted with the help of the smaller kids, who dropped the seeds in the holes. Those too young to pick cotton put boll weevils in a Coke bottle for a penny apiece. Children also shelled butterbeans, which Matt sold door-to-door from his truck.

"Fresh shelled butterbeans," he would say as he drove past the houses of mostly White people.

Soon people dropped by to purchase these items, and Matt kept adding things to sell from the house. This was the genesis of Matt's first grocery store that was started in a small building in the fork of the road.

The Big House had two small houses next door that looked like slave or servant quarters, one of which Murrh and Pap moved into with their dog Callo. It became a family tradition to have relatives or guests live with the Nelms. When Rena's brother Bert married Lizzie Mae, they lived with Matt and Rena for a while in the Big House, perhaps a payback for helping Matt to marry Rena. Mother Staten moved in with them for almost a year but always longed for her independence. Believe it or not, she started to build her own house and got as far as the foundation before her health failed and she gave up the idea.

One frequent house guest was Rena's friend Sallie, who was said to talk like an "African." Evidently no one in the country knew what that meant, since Sallie was from the island of "Buford," South Carolina and the Gullah language was responsible for that reputation. The children called her "Miss Sallie," which was kind of unusual, since close friends who took on the characteristics of a relative were called "aunts and uncles" not "miss and mister." Sallie made a beautiful quilt for Rena with every patch perfectly straight and every stitch the same size with beautiful red and green colors that spread out from the center. The children called it "the peacock quilt." It disappeared and rumor had it that Rena's Aunt Louise, caught rummaging through Rena's things, took it.

Another of Rena's friends named Becka was a frequent visitor who earned the designation of "aunt." When Aunt Becka came, she helped Rena bake all kinds of cakes and pies, told fascinating stories, and played with all the children. She was fun to be around, and no one treated her differently because she was blind, and she liked it that way. Aunt Becka and her sister Lucille, who was never elevated to the status of an "aunt," lived on Beecham Street in Tisdell. The girls, who went to the private school in Tisdell (none of the boys attended), sometimes stayed overnight with Aunt Becka.

After leaving the Big House about 1945, Matt bought a home and acquired a huge tract of land on Tisdell road about seven miles farther east toward the city. The house was on top of a hill and he built a general store across the road from the home. Geneva, born in this house in 1946, was delivered by Miss Pleutsy, but the last child, Rebecca, was born in the Black section of the Tisdell hospital two years later. People in the country were beginning to believe that giving birth in hospitals was safer than using midwives. A contributing factor was that Matt's brother Walton's wife, Mary, died giving birth to their second child, a breech baby the midwife couldn't deliver. By the time they got to the hospital, they both had died. Many people remembered the event, because Mary played the piano at different church events. Around her house she could even be heard playing and singing the blues, particularly when Uncle Walton made her angry. When she was in one of those moods, you could find her on the piano playing and singing her favorite song: "Baby I'm leaving, for the big city I'm bound. If you don't believe I'm going, just count the days I'm gone."

The death of Aunt Mary was an event that presaged a decade of Nelms family tragedy. Matt's son Andrew received a head injury in a car accident returning from taking a friend home. He was taken to the Tisdell hospital, where he was patched up and released. During the night, his condition worsened and he had to be taken back to the hospital. He later died from a bacterial infection or meningitis, caused by improper bandaging. Elizabeth, home for the funeral, went to the hospital to complain, but nothing became of it.

Still, she insisted, "God punishes ugly. We don't know when or how, but God always punishes ugly."

Matt's sister Eulala, who lived in Tisdell, worked at Grant's Mill operating an open elevator that brought cotton from the building's loft to the spinning room. A bale of cotton fell on top of her head and broke her neck. She died in the hospital two days later. Turner, Matt's brother, was hit and killed by a drunk driver while helping to pave Ramsey Road, but the worst family tragedy occurred when Nathan Crawley killed Uncle Jake's son John during a fight. The next day, Jake caught up with Crawley and shot him in the face with a 12-gauge shotgun. He drew a life sentence in prison for premeditated murder even though he was defended by a prominent White attorney who claimed the Bible allowed "an eye for an eye." Uncle Jake's other son, Listervelt, lived with Matt and Rena after Jake's imprisonment.

In 1956, Matt built a modern house about fifty yards behind the old house on the hill. Uncle Nate, a bachelor and a veteran, stayed in the old house until he came home drunk one night and burned the house down by smoking in bed. The new house where Matt and Rena spent the rest of their lives was white with asbestos siding, a big picture window, two porches (a front one for show and a well-used one on the east side), running water from a pump in the well, and an indoor bathroom the girls treated as their personal property. A wood heater—there was no fireplace—was in the center of the living room that jokingly became central heat. As one walked in the front door, there was a living room with a small kitchen off to the right with an electric stove, a refrigerator, and a laundry room with a washer. Rena continued to dry her clothes outside because she said they needed the fresh air. There were three bedrooms, one for Matt and Rena, one for the boys, and one for the girls. Everybody still shared a room, but by that time only the twins and two younger girls were at home.

Mt. Canaan was the school the Nelms children attended and Miss Tara Williams, the first college-educated teacher born in the country, was the teacher. Miss Williams recalled that when Lonnie and Ronnie were too young to attend school, they used to run to meet her without a stitch of clothing. Black children walked to school in the South in all kinds of weather. The first one (student or teacher) to arrive made a fire in the stove. Teresa remembered that White children wondered why they did not go to school with them.

"On the last time we stayed in the big house, we had some White kids that would come over and stay on our porch to catch the school bus, and *we had to walk to school.* They asked us why we did not catch the bus and go to school with them. That was in the forties, 1940-41. I told them we was not allowed because we was Colored. They did not understand that, so I said 'because our skin was darker than y'all.'"

White children were born free of race prejudice, *tabula rasa,* but they acquired bigotry subliminally. In other words, it was unnecessary for White parents to teach hatred to their children. Children needed only to observe them and interact with an environment replete with symbols of Black subjugation. By adolescence, White children no longer wondered why they did not go to school with Black children; custom had replaced innocence. By the time they reached high school, they were fully vested. Those who owned cars now threw Coke bottles out of their windows at Black school children walking home without fear of consequences.

On the other hand, Black parents in the country had to teach their children about racism, but unlike city life, there was no daily encounter with segregation's racial etiquette. The Nelms children were more exposed to Jim Crow than other children because of Matt's store. His children recalled that he used metaphors to explain how to identify racial boundaries and avoid racial land-mines. Racism, for example, was just one more of life's rivers to cross. Whites, he explained, would help a Black friend across on a boat, but would not build a bridge for him to cross on his own. He also said segregation was like a pasture that fenced in Black folks who had to work within its boundaries. His favorite meta-phor was that racism was like cow dung—it looked hard, but when you stepped on it, it was all mushy inside. In other words, White people were not always what they seemed to be, and they could turn on you when you didn't expect it.

Matt encouraged his children to be pragmatic, to work within these constraints, but he occasionally pushed the racial envelope. He was what might be called a "passive passer," one that did not claim to be White, but didn't correct those who assumed he was when it was to his advantage. That was the case when he and the boys visited the stockyard, about twice a month on Thursdays. The stockyard looked like an athletic arena, with long seats like church pews that extended about fifty feet on both sides facing each other east and west, with this giant area between them. It had a large door on the south side where the stock—cows, hogs, horses, goats, and so on—were brought in for sale. After the auc-tion, they went out a door on the north side where they were put in these holding cells near the loading docks.

There weren't any signs that designated seats for "Colored" or "White," but it was customary for the few Black people to sit in a small area on the west side. One time, Matt sat on the White side with his son Andrew, who was asked to leave, but Matt said, "he is a good boy," and they let him stay. On this Thursday in the mid-1950s, the twins went to the stockyard with him.

After a couple of hours of browsing, Matt told the boys, "nothing jumps out at me today."

They decided to get something to eat before leaving for home. A few blocks away, a Black man called Big Shorty ran a barbecue stand where they often went to eat, but today Matt decided to get the beef and potato soup and a bottle of hot sauce from the stockyard kitchen. It was about 11:00 a.m. and the lines were going to be long, as people wanted to eat before the auction started at noon. Matt left the boys in the truck and thought he might use the line for Whites. He was a little reluctant, but this guy saw him looking around and pointed him toward the White folks' line, thus making the decision for him. It was the practice at the stockyard to serve all hungry White folks before serving any Blacks. After about ten minutes Matt reached the front of the line.

"What's your pleasure?" the waiter asked.

Maybe it wasn't a good day for buying cattle, but Matt felt an urge to be recalcitrant after surveying the lines where five Black people waited for twenty Whites to get a barbecue sandwich.

"I'm sorry, maybe you can serve that Colored man while I make up my mind," Matt responded.

As a matter of fact, Matt recognized the Black man in front of the line as Ben Johnson and believed that Ben also recognized him.

"Don't be smart, Mack—we don't serve Negroes until Whites are waited on." He scared Matt for a split second because he thought he said Matt.

"I'm still deciding," Matt said.

At this point, two or three Whites behind Matt started to grumble. One said:

"Negroes wait until Whites are done, not the other way

around,"

"Where you from?" another mumbled.

The manager of the restaurant came in to see what the fuss was all about. After he determined the situation, he looked at Matt, glanced at the handful of Blacks, and called Joe from the kitchen. Joe, a big Black guy about 6 feet 6 inches, came in wearing a filthy apron and a white sweat rag around his neck. Matt thought at first that he was going to be kicked out by this guy, but realized that would be ridiculous—White people didn't get Black people to bounce out White people, forgetting briefly that he was not White.

"Joe, serve them Coloreds there and then go back to the kitchen," the manager instructed him.

Joe bowed his head as he ran over to the other line to serve the Black customers.

"I'll take three large soups, three corn breads, three teas and a big bottle of hot sauce," Matt said.

Matt had rebelled in a small way against an unjust system, but a firm punishment awaited any of his children who pulled such a stunt.

Chapter 4

GHOSTLORE IN THE FAMILY

Did you see that? Did you see t-h-a-t?
Did you s-e-e t-h-a-t? Did y-o-u s-e-e
t-h-a-t? D-i-d y-o- - -

Gus the Ghost

*M*att's attention to the children was special, given that he lived in an era when nurturing was a maternal function. He allowed kids to have the run of the store, took them out for long rides, taught them to drive when their feet could barely reach the pedals, and played games with them. He particularly liked to tell his children stories about ghosts, especially in the winter in front of the heater or fireplace while everybody ate peanuts, pecans, or sweet potatoes cooked in the fireplace. He talked about ghosts every time he got a chance, usually to instruct the children as well as to entertain them. He told them ghosts lived in the attic of the Big House to keep them out of the Lambs' possessions. Whether he realized it or not, he was paying homage to his West African ancestors who believed that the spirits of the dead influenced the living and dwelled among them in the community.

Many of the children who are much older now have recollections of Matt's story-telling, though some of the details of the stories have faded from memory. Of course, any person who truly believes can see a ghost, and some animals, especially cats with nine lives, can see them. Rebecca said that she used to see "haunts" when she was a little girl. This happened when she fell asleep at the store and Matt carried her up the hill in his arms. It was then she would see the ghosts mostly of animals, like cows and horses, but no people.

Only Matt believed she saw anything, even though, according to him, it was more difficult for children to see ghosts than it was for old people because they were farther away from being one. Perhaps that's why Rebecca only saw animals, but they went away when she got older. When a young person frequently saw ghosts, some considered it a curse or bad omen.

Although ghost stories are rarely told today, some of them are still vivid in the memories of family members. One such story was that when Matt was a small boy, he and some other boys about his age used to run alongside and catch up with the freight train that ran through Nelms County late afternoons during the week and about noon on Saturdays. If the train were going slowly, they would run faster than the train and cross the track in front of it. They knew the danger, but it was done mostly on a dare – boys would try almost anything on a dare, even climb to the top of the tallest tree. On this particular Saturday, the noon train was going faster than usual. The boys—Matt, Gus, Rufus, Johnnie, and Hobie—ran alongside it anyway. They could run fast enough to get past it, but doubted if they could get far enough in front of it to cross the tracks safely. All the boys except Gus realized this and refused to take the chance on crossing. Gus was faster and older than the other boys and decided that he could get up enough speed to cross the track anyway. He prized his hard-earned reputation as the speediest boy in the group. Although he had outrun the other boys in every past contest, he thought nothing would solidify his status more than to jump across this one, since the other boys were obviously scared to try.

Sensing what Gus was up to as they ran alongside the train, Matt yelled "no Gus, its going too fast, we know you are faster than us!" Matt begged him not to try what he was thinking.

"I can do it. I can do it," Gus claimed as he picked up speed and got just in front of the engine compartment of the speeding train.

"N O O O O Gus, don't, don't," pleaded the boys. "It's going too fast," they screamed.

The boys could now see the engineer in the train car's window yelling at them and blowing his whistle for them to get away from the tracks. They really didn't know what the engineer was saying, since they could not hear him, but whatever it was, he was saying it with great agitation.

"You ain't go make it," Hobie screamed at Gus in a final warning with his bass-filled voice.

Gus ran faster and managed to get four, maybe five yards just ahead of the train. He, like the other boys, knew that this was not far enough to get across safely. Gus reached back for a last burst of speed, pulled about ten yards in front of the train, then attempted to put one foot on the railroad track to use it as a lever to spring himself across the track to the other side. Unfortunately, Gus missed the rail and fell down head first in front of the train. His head was severed as cleanly from his body as if it had been cleaved by the guillotine, and Gus's body lay limp just along the railroad track. His head went rolling down the hillside.

"Did you see that? Did you see that?" Gus's head inquired as it rolled down the hill alongside the train. "Did you s-e-e t-h-a-t? D-i-d y-o-u- s-e-e- t-h-a-t-? Did y-o-u s-e-e ...."

Finally, the boys heard nothing. Matt and the others stood beside the headless body in shock, but not too traumatized to wonder how they would explain this thing to the old folks as they pondered what punishment they had coming, but mostly they just felt sorry for Gus. Johnnie went down and found Gus' head at the foot of the hill, since he thought it would be needed for the funeral. He had a difficult time convincing Matt and the others—Hobie had already run home—to help him bring it back up the hill. Black people, you know, can't go to heaven during resurrection without all their body parts. If Gus's head had not been found, he would have had to roam throughout eternity barred from heaven or something awful like that, because he was headless.

Needless to say, the boys were whipped severely. Matt's grandmother beat him so badly with a rope that he couldn't go to school, because he couldn't sit down. The boys never knew whether the engineer realized what happened, since there was no formal hearing or anything that they knew anything about. The sheriff came and asked some questions – he said for the records. The children understood he didn't care, so they didn't tell him anything. It was bad enough that they had to live with those words imprinted indelibly in their minds:

"Did you see that? D-i-d y-o-u s-e-e-e t-h-a-a-t?"

The funeral was one of the saddest ever remembered in Nelms County. Black folk generally had a festive time at funerals, because they called them home-goings for the deceased (home-comings for the living since everybody comes home from up north), but this was different; this was a kid who died for a dumb reason. There was even a moratorium on drinking at funerals, though that was short-lived and not universally observed. Somehow the mortician managed to repair Gus's face, sew Gus's head back on his body, and with the suit and tie buttoned around Gus's neck, one could not tell the head had been severed.

According to Matt, some nights, perhaps about once a month, he would leave the store to walk up the hill to the house, which was about a tenth of a mile away, and Gus would wait for him. Gus always walked along a while before he said anything. Then he would attempt conversation by asking Matt, "Did you see that?" "Did you see that?" That's how he knew it was Gus instead of some other ghost. Matt never said anything and they just walked along together. Gus always ended his visit at the door and never asked to come inside. Maybe Matt told this story to stop his children from taking unnecessary risks or being goaded into bad things.

When the Nelms family lived in what the children remember as "the sticks," Matt told many tales—that's what some folks called them. There was one ghost story he told about a haunted house about a mile away where a lady stayed all by herself. She was making bread one evening and cat came in and he was helping her make the bread; he started licking her finger and saying, "nobody here but us cats." He was eating her finger.

Hattie remembered that her father told the story for a purpose. "One time while Daddy was telling us this story, when a cat came in our house. We had a cat—Crack, we called him—but all of us, about five of us girls, jumped all over Daddy's lap because it was not our cat. He enjoyed scaring us girls so that we would cling to him."

Of course, everybody knows cats are close to ghosts because with so many lives they have been there. You can see a cat jump up and go after things in a room that nobody sees or he scurries out of the room because a ghost is present.

Another story Matt told was about his friend Joe Fred Brown, who drowned while fishing in the Eucheche Creek near his house. Joe was awfully afraid of the water and could not swim, so Matt always wondered why he went fishing at all. A water moccasin, the people were told, crawled up Joe's pants leg and scared Joe so badly that he fell into the creek and drowned. Matt said that whenever he drove past Eucheche Creek, Joe hitched a ride on his truck. He could hear a clunk as Joe jumped on the running board.

"Hey Matt, how you today?" Joe would say.

"Doing fine Joe, how you?" Matt would respond.

He knew this was Joe because of where he jumped on the truck, just as he knew Gus by what he said. That was all the conversation they would have for the next six miles or so, when he came to the abandoned house where Joe used to live and he got off the truck.

"See you, Matt," Joe would say.

Sometimes when Matt returned, Joe would hop back on the truck.

"Going fishing, Joe?" Matt would ask.

"Yeah, here dey biting real good," Joe responded.

Matt never explained why he talked to Joe but not to Gus. It was also not clear why he told this story. If it had a moral beyond being careful, it was elusive.

Matt told his children that there were good ghosts and bad ghosts. Some ghosts, he said, were playful like children, but those who died young, like Gus, became bitter as time passed because they were deprived of so many opportunities. They sometimes felt deprived of pleasures that they never experienced in life and became jealous of humans because they had bodies. For example, a ghost who liked chocolate might enter the body of someone eating chocolate in order that he could taste it, or a ghost like Joe could have entered Matt's body to experience what it was like to drive a truck.

Ghosts sometimes showed up with a distinct purpose, like keeping a relative or friend out of trouble or to warn a relative of impending disaster. Most ghosts, however, just played and hung around, according to Matt, and got into mischief out of boredom. The word "poltergeist" was not in Matt's vocabulary, but he was not the type to use a big word when a little word would do. When people went out to work or to church, playful ghosts changed things around or hid things so you couldn't find them when you came back. They also moved furniture around—like chairs and tables, or rearranged kitchen utensils and dishes, which they left on the table as if they had had a meal. Sometimes ghosts would take items away and bring them back later when you didn't expect it. That's why old folks "back in the day" didn't like to be told that they didn't leave an object where they said or had not done something when they knew that they had done it. At that time, old people were not so casually told they were demented, because everybody believed ghosts did devious things. Today, nobody believes in ghosts, so the elderly don't get the benefit of the doubt. When they complain that someone has messed with their medicines, for example, a young person thinks they are losing it without even considering the possibility that a ghost might be responsible.

Ghosts were closer to old people anyway, according to Matt, because they were soon to be one of them. Indeed, the older a ghost got, the more powerful he became. Joe was always a good ghost, but Gus, who died before his time and roamed around, became a bad ghost the older he got. Ghosts, Matt said, were "haunts" when they became bad. In most cases, an individual's personality in life followed him or her to ghosthood, but in some cases the nature of the death could alter a spirit's personality, as with Gus. As time passed, the more Gus resented dying at such a young age, his bitterness and power grew commensurately and people started blaming him for some awful things. When beautiful cousin Amanda was burned badly in a house fire, some said it wasn't God that punished her for her vanity, but it was Gus who set the fire and caused this evil deed that disfigured her so badly.

Ghosts were social beings like living people, since they liked to hang out in groups. A large group of ghosts was the "cemetery ghosts" because that was the place where many hung out. That's why it was so difficult for pastors to get Black people to help keep their burial grounds cleaned up. Another group of ghosts were known as "witch ghosts," who rode people at night in their sleep. While being ridden by one of these ghosts, the person is completely immobilized and cannot move until the witch ghost has reached his or her destination or someone shakes you and forces him or her off of you. Then you stay awake for a while to make sure another one does not hitch a ride. Anyone who has been ridden by a witch ghost can attest to what a terribly helpless feeling it is.

There was another set of bad ghosts called "bridge men" who shunned the cemetery and hid out under bridges and overpasses. They weren't real bad, just mischievous. When you were traveling in a wagon or even a car at night and tried to cross a bridge, they would grab the tires and wheels and hold them so you couldn't move. That was their favorite pastime, holding the tires of cars or wagons of people who tried to cross bridges. After a while, they would let go of the wheels and wager on how long a person would remain after they had released the vehicle.

Matt explained to his children that being broke was a sin, since it resulted from laziness, and told them that ghosts hated broke people and messed with those who did not keep money. He told them that you could be walking down the road and suddenly be slapped in the face and look up and nobody was there. People who got broke from gambling, drinking, or something like that made ghosts insult them quicker. Matt told his children that the only way to keep the haunts off them was to always carry money and he gave them nickels, dimes, or quarters, depending on their age, to keep the ghosts off them.

"If you lose all this money or spend it, all the ghosts will get you," Matt said.

Sometimes he would put a coin in one hand behind his back, then return both hands closed and ask you to guess the hand the coin was in. If you guessed correctly, you got to keep the money to stave off the ghosts. Later, he would ask you to show him some money, and if you didn't have any, he would quickly jump away from you, saying he didn't want to be near you when the ghost got you. As a result, his children always worked or ran businesses so they could have money, avoiding being broke even in the age of credit cards. These stories had a lifetime impact.

Some people claimed they could communicate with ghosts

and derived their powers from being around them. Matt's store was about a quarter of a mile from the Mt. Canaan Missionary Baptist Church, so he had the responsibility of looking out for the church in case of thieves or vandals, if you can believe that people would actually steal from or destroy a church. One night, Matt saw the church lights on inside the sanctuary and decided that when he closed the store he would go down and turn out the lights, since he thought somebody had just forgotten to turn them off. By the time he closed the store, however, the church lights were already off. The next night, a Thursday, he saw the lights on again, but at closing time they were off again. On Friday, he decided to check it out as soon as they came on to see what was going on. When he arrived at the church, he saw a red motorcycle with huge red saddle bags sitting beside the steps of the church. Matt was a little afraid, since nobody he knew rode a motorcycle; certainly there was no Black person in Nelms County in those days who owned a motorcycle, and even if someone did own one, it would not have been this devil red color. Matt did not carry a weapon—he didn't even own a handgun, just two shotguns, a 12-gauge single barrel and a 16-gauge double barrel, which were used for hunting. He considered returning to the store to borrow a pistol from Kalem, but thought better of the idea.

"Why would anyone who wanted to do harm to somebody be inside of a church?" Matt reasoned.

He entered the sanctuary, where he could only see the back of a man who must have been nine feet tall standing in front of the pulpit. When Matt got closer, he saw this extremely pale man standing on the front pew, which made him look two or three feet taller than he was. He was staring at the cross hanging over the back of the pulpit. He had to be a White man to be that pale, but he looked like one of those Albinos, Matt thought, he was so pale. Matt had never seen an Albino, but guessed that must have been what he was. This Albino was ill clad, with a long coat that looked like a cape, and his feet were wet, as he stood there straight as an arrow just staring at the cross beyond the pulpit.

Matt tried to explain to the pale man that he could not stay in the church, but every time Matt started to talk, the man raised both his hands high in the air for him to be quiet. The Albino then dropped his arms to his sides, outstretched to resemble a cross, while he continued to stare transfixed at the big cross. Matt tried again and the man again raised his hands for silence. This time, Matt noticed that the tips of the man's fingers were as red as fire and seemed swollen to the point that they would burst from the slightest prick. This was no ordinary dude, he mused.

Matt decided to give the Albino some time to finish whatever he was doing, so he walked around to see if anything was missing from the church. Everything seemed to be in place, but outside he saw where the man had gotten his feet wet by trouncing around in the cemetery. When he retraced the Albino's footsteps, Matt discovered that the man had not been trouncing randomly, but that his footprints formed several large crosses.

Matt returned to the sanctuary where the Albino looked even more like a ghost. It was like he was in a meditation so deep that it was sucking the color from him or draining the blood from his system. The deeper the meditation, it seemed, the more blood it required and the paler the Albino became. Matt decided that the Albino could hear him and he would make his point, outstretched hands, meditation, or not.

"Mister, you can't stay here, and if you are not gone by tomorrow morning, I will call the sheriff," Matt said emphatically, ignoring the man's outstretched arms call for silence.

The next day, which was a Saturday, just before noon the Albino showed up at Matt's store, still looking like a ghost, which frightened the children who saw him. There was a number of people in the store doing their business who now stopped to observe this strange sight. In a few minutes, the children got over their fear and found the red motorcycle more fascinating than the Albino. The man never gave his name, but told Matt he had completed his "regeneration." He apologized for any inconvenience he might have caused and said that he was leaving for Tisdell where he had some engagements.

"What do you mean, re-gener, ah, regeneration?" Matt stumbled.

"I draw my strength from communicating with the dead, the spirits. A cross is the conduit and the large ones in churches are the best channels. I contact the dead for those who wish to hear from their friends and family, I am a spiritualist. It is from the dead that I derive my powers. I suppose my regeneration can be likened to the man next door [pointing to Kalem's garage] recharging a battery in a car," the ghost said.

"The ghost"—only Matt still believed he was an Albino—saw so many people staring at him that he could tell they were not believers in his alleged spiritualism. He decided to do a demonstration of his regenerated powers and asked Matt for the piece of rope which he had spotted hanging on the wall. Matt handed it to him. After closing his eyes, mumbling something several times, and slithering the rope through his hands and fingers, he gave it back to Matt. He looked over at Henry Greenblatt, a frequent customer, who was standing in the corner, and asked Matt to tie the rope securely around Henry's neck, which Matt accomplished only after much reluctance from Henry. The pale man asked others to verify that the knot Matt had tied was secure. When all were satisfied that the knot would not come loose, the ghost moved over to Henry, closed his eyes briefly, and tapped Henry on top of the head five or six times like he was unloosing the top of a mayonnaise jar. As the ghost tapped on Henry's head, Henry's eyes closed and his face lost all expression. The ghost then repeated a few words in a language that no one understood except perhaps the devil himself. He then grabbed a handful of

Henry's hair to lift his head and neck four or five inches above his shoulders. The ghost slowly pulled the rope through the opening between Henry's neck and shoulders so that people could actually see it coming through and knew they were not being tricked by some sleight-of-hand.

He handed the rope to Matt who, along with several others, examined the knot and determined that it had been undisturbed. When all were satisfied, the Albino carefully sat Henry's head back on his shoulders. He again tapped on top of Henry's head several times, a little harder than the first time, as Henry's eyes re-opened and the expression returned to his face. The pale man left the store with all in utter disbelief at what they had witnessed, or thought they had witnessed, and rode off on his motorcycle. All that could be seen as the ghost left was his overcoat flying in the wind. This is a true story, as all witnesses will attest, and Henry swears even now, years later. that his head feels like it's going to roll off his shoulders, if he isn't careful.

Chapter 5
GAMES, GIRLS, AND GUYS

> There is no great sorrow damned up
> in my soul… I do not belong to the
> sobbing school of Negrohood who
> hold that nature somehow has given
> them a lowdown dirty deal.
>
> Zora Neale Hurston[4]

Children who lived in the country had many chores to do, since a strong work ethic was part of growing up country. Matt's boys cut firewood, drew water, fed the cows and hogs, and worked in the field and grocery store. The girls did some of these things too, but they mostly worked in the house and store. Both preferred working in the store to being in the field, since they could eat candy and ice cream and share it with their friends. The boys even had their own mini-businesses peddling vegetables, selling flower seeds, and distributing *Grit* newspapers. Like Matt, they had "employees" who performed their chores like cutting firewood in exchange for items taken from the store. Neither Matt nor Rena considered it stealing, but if caught, they could be whipped for lying about it. By the time the twins were teenagers, Matt's major businesses were running the store and operating a pulpwood business, having abandoned his aspirations for a huge farm for a few acres to raise mostly vegetables. On Saturdays, holidays, and during the summer Lonnie and Ronnie had to cut limbs from trees, mark the logs for cutting, and help load the trucks.

Performing chores did not prevent children from playing a

variety of games, mostly outside. When children were very small, Matt played a game with them by pulling their toes, starting with the big one and ending with the little one.

"This little piggy wants some corn, this little piggy says where are you going to get it? This little piggy says out de barn, this little piggy says I'll tell, and this little piggy says 'twee, twee,'" squeezing the little toe to get a reaction or sound from the child.

One can only guess that this was a slave game, since the barn probably belonged to the master and the little toe was a squealer—perhaps a house slave. Black parents did not tell their offspring they could be anything they wanted to be, but children who wanted to escape played "make believe" which allowed them to do something they could not do, be something they could not be, or own something they could not afford. They could live in mansions, drive big cars, and hold important positions. Perhaps this form of escapism allowed them to pursue the American dream decreed to every White child by the nation's founders but denied to Black children.

Some games were played by either girls or boys, but gender monopolies were a function of attitudes rather than ability. Jacks or jackstones was a favorite game that was played inside and outside mostly by girls. A player threw down jacks or stones and then threw up a small ball while picking up the stones in sequence (one, then two, then three etc.) on the first bounce of the ball. Another girls' game was hopscotch, which was played in the yard on a cross of squares drawn on the ground. A player threw a coin or rock for example in a square and had to go through each square in sequence on one foot, picking up the coin. The object was to get through all the squares one at a time, without putting both feet on the ground or stepping on unacceptable squares.

Girls played several ring games like Ring Around the Rosies, where they joined hands and went around in a circle with one girl within the circle. They sang:

Ring around the rosies,
Pocket full of toe-sies,
Light bread, sweet bread
Squat!

The last person to squat was the loser and replaced the person in the circle. Of course, there was always plenty of controversy, since it was a rare occasion where the last person to squat was clearly identifiable. A discussion led to a decision as to who was last to squat, and girls would lose friends for almost a week over these choices. If any good came of this game it was because of the lessons in democracy, compromise, and give-and-take.

Another ring game was Little Sally Walker, where the players got in a circle with one person in the middle squatting down while they sang a song. As they sang the person in the circle imitated what was sung:

Little Sally Walker,
Sitting in a saucer,
Crying and weeping over all she done done.
Rise, Sally, rise,
Wipe your weeping eyes.
Fly to the east,
Fly to the west,
Fly to the very one you love the best.

The game seemed to vary from time to time, though it's hard to recall exactly how and why. It seems that if the girls knew another girl had a crush on a certain boy, they turned to that boy, if present, the girl in the circle had a crush on. Recollections vary, but sometimes they replaced "turn to the east or west" with "shake it to the east, shake it to the west," where they shook their butts.

It seems that there was a line before "their butts" that said, "put your hands on your hips, let your backbone slip" and they stuck out their behinds.

Another of these games was "Ant Dinah's Dead" which was a game played when all the players formed a circle with one person in the center of the circle who played out the description in the song:

1. Aunt Dinah's Dead (the leader says)
Oh, how did she die? (the group asks)
Oh, she died like this,
(Leader imitated how she died)
Oh, she died like this,
(Group makes a pose)
(They then repeat the above)
2. Aunt Dinah's Living (Leader)
Oh, how did she live? (Group)
Oh, she lived in the country (All act out the following)
"Till she moved downtown,
She's gonna shimmy, shimmy,
shimmy till the sun goes
down. She pulled up her
dress, above her knees.
She never went to college,
she never went to school,
but when she got the boogie,
she's an educated fool.

Another of these games was called Lost My Handkerchief Yesterday. A group of children made a circle with one person walking around behind the group with a handkerchief or object and drops it behind a child's back while they sang.

I lost my handkerchief yesterday,
I found it again today.
I found it full of buttermilk,
and dripped it all the way.
Drip, drop, drip, drop, and so on.

That player then tried to catch the person who dropped it. If the person wasn't caught, the child dropped it behind another person's back.

Boys played marbles when they weren't hunting, fishing, riding car tires, or playing baseball. It was not unusual to see them with pockets full of marbles that they had acquired by "playing for keeps." The game was played by placing marbles randomly inside a circle drawn on the ground and taking a marble called the shooter and using it to knock an opponent's marbles out the ring, while keeping your shooter inside the circle. If a player failed to propel a marble from the circle or his shooter landed outside the ring, the boy lost his term. Robert Arnett, a stocky boy called "Stumpy," was the best player. He got down on his elbows and took his shooter—a big black marble—and knocked all your marbles out of the ring before you got a chance to play. Nobody played "for keeps" with Stumpy.

Boys also played a game called Red Rover. They drew a line on the ground and formed two groups; one group of boys would line up along the line and lock each other by the hands and arms. The other set of boys lined up several yards away in front of them. The boys who were locked in arms would huddle together to choose someone from the other side to try to break the lock. In unison they would sing, "Red Rover, Red Rover, send Benny over." Then the chosen youngster, in this case Benny, would run as fast and hard as he could into the line to try to break through. If he failed, he rejoined his group, but a successful boy could join the line of interlocked boys. There was a danger in trying too hard to break the line, because the boys would conspire beforehand that when a certain name was called they would release the lock as the boy hurtled his way through the air and allowed him to land flat on his face.

Mostly girls jumped rope (sometimes alone, but other times as many as three at a time) but a boy could do it without being labeled a "sissy." They both played dodge ball, a game that should be self-explanatory. A game that had no name was called "ball over the house" where a ball was thrown over the top of a house and when someone from the other side caught the ball the players ran to exchange sides; if caught the player was hit with the ball. If the ball failed to get over the house, it was announced that "leg got broke." Houses were not underpinned in those days, so children could often see where other players were by looking under the house and watching their feet.

There were no movie houses or theaters in Nelms County for Blacks or Whites during the Jim Crow era. In the early years Matt's house was one of the places in the community with a radio, and people would come by to listen to programs, like the fights. Later, there was a very popular radio station coming out of Nashville, Tennessee, that many Blacks listened to that had a disc jockey (DJ) named Robert R who played the Blues and other favorite Black tunes. There was a consensus among Black people in the country that he was Black, since no White man would play this kind of music, but it turns out the consensus was erroneous. By the time most people had radios, they came out with television. Kalem bought the first television set in the community sometime in the early 1950s, and he allowed neighbors to gather at his house to watch.

Blacks from the country often went to the all-Black Union Theater in Tisdell, which was a real nice place that had seats downstairs and upstairs. Some Tisdell Blacks went downtown to a White movie house where they had to go around to the back and climb up the fire escape and sit in the balcony. Black people from the country never went to the White theater. They preferred the Union, which was owned and operated by a Black man who was a medical doctor. It not only featured motion pictures but entertainers (singers and comedians) and boxing matches. The Union had this rather large sign out front with a light over it that said: "COLORED ONLY: No Whites Allowed." Here was a place with a sign that kept Whites out, which was fascinating to the young people from the country, since all the signs they encountered in Nelms County had "Whites Only: No Colored Allowed." Perhaps that's why the doctor had his sign made up like that and named it the Union.

Sometimes Kalem allowed the boys—Junior, Lonnie and Ronnie—to transform his garage into a movie house. His son Junior, or Lil Kal, named for his father, moved out all the cars while Lonnie and Ronnie pushed all the tools to the back of the building and put in folding chairs for seats. The chairs were placed in rows of about twelve that made the garage look like a theater, since the concrete floor of the garage was built on an incline to drain water; it became lower as one moved toward the back of the shop where the oil pit was located and the movie screen was set up there to accommodate the 16mm movie projector. Junior ordered the movies from mail-order houses in New York or California. The boys acted as ushers and charged a nickel or dime for admission. The audience, not knowing any better, cheered for cowboys and Confederates—Lash Larue, Tex Ritter, John Wayne, Alan Ladd and others—who killed Indians and battled Yankee crooks. There were no westerns that featured Black heroes, just buffoons. No one had heard about the outlaw Deadwood Dick, sheriff Bass Reeves, or military heroes like the Buffalo Soldiers.

Boys themselves played cowboys and Indians with BB guns, slingshots, and pop guns. Slingshots were easily made with a piece of forked limb, some rubber from an old inner tube and a piece of leather, say from a shoe tongue, to hold the projectile. The pop guns were harder to make. To make one, the boys got some hollow bamboo from somewhere near the creek, stripped the bark from a piece of tree limb for a handle, shaped it to size, and oiled it just enough that it would slide through the bamboo, where a chinaberry was stuck in the opposite end. When the handle was pushed through the bamboo, the air would compress, forcing the chinaberry from its covering and from the gun at an amazing speed. It hurt badly if you got hit with one. Lil Kal was always ahead of the curve. He made the best pop guns and slingshots and when other boys had to cock their BB guns he had a Daisy pump. When the other boys got bicycles, he had a ten-speed Schwinn. He was also first to own a car, a 1954 Chevy on the outside, a Pontiac under the hood.

Being bad in those days was not serious. Boys just did little things, like stealing tomatoes from a neighbor's garden or sneaking off to the creek to fish to avoid chopping wood. They also liked finding ways to scare or embarrass the girls, like sitting next to one in school and cupping their arm pit to make an "arm fart." When the nurse administered vaccinations or shots, the students lined up in the hallway leading to the Jeanes Supervisor's office and the older boys would rush to the head of the line to take their shots first. Before exiting, they would squeeze their arms to make them bleed to scare the girls and the squeamish boys. Perhaps the most notorious thing they did at school was to bring a piece of a broken a mirror from home and tie it to the top of their shoes at lunchtime and stick their feet under a girl's dress so that they could see her panties. Such a thing was a prank in those days, but now it's a sexual offense.

When teenagers began to think about dating, their thoughts turned to more important issues, like hair care. Most of Matt's and Rena's girls had "good hair," but those whose hair was "nappy" had quite a time with the hot iron, which left little burn spots on their necks and scalps. The boys' hair was cut twice a month by Matt's friend Deacon Walter Denton, who was so big that he could hardly reach beyond his stomach to your head. He also used these dull manual clippers with handles that he worked like scissors. What was already a "mammy made" haircut that you were ashamed of was made worse because you jerked your head around in pain, leaving these clean spots in your hair. The boys preferred to go to Hamp's Barber Shop in Tisdell, located on 13th Street where they played checkers, drank Cokes, and ate candy. Mr. Hamp had sharp electric clippers that hummed and he never left clean spots in your hair. A few blocks away on the same street, there was a female barber who cut the boys' hair on rare occasions when Matt didn't have time to wait for Mr. Hamp. Her name was "Miss Chester" and she was a member of the House of Prayer, which held large parades when the leader, Daddy Grace, came to town.

The main attraction of adults in the country was the juke or jook, which was as much a part of the culture as church, checkers and baseball. On Friday and Saturday nights people shot pool (billiards), listened to music, danced to the music of a DJ, ate barbecue, and those who were of a mind to drank and gambled. When there was no Disc Jockey, music was played on the "piccolo" or jukebox. People inserted coins and chose recordings by such artists as Slim Harpo, Muddy Waters, Lightning Hopkins, and other favorites. Jukes didn't usually have fancy names like the clubs in Tisdell, but they attracted customers from the city. Boys tried to keep girls in their neighborhood from dating boys in other communities, but country boys particularly disliked losing a girl to a city boy. Exacerbating the situation was the female idiosyncrasy of showing more interest in strangers than the homegrown variety.

The quality of these places, as well as the kind of people they attracted, reflected the character of the owner. Kalem ran one of the most popular and peaceful joints in the country. Its closest competitor was a place called Foreman's, though the owner called it The Full Moon. Foreman's was located off the main road about four miles down a country road with a frequently used u-turn for drivers who lost the debate with their dates about the direction to take their relationships. Those who made it to the juke could see the Savannah River at the end of the road, where an iron bar with a stop sign in the middle prevented a drunk from driving past Foreman's smack dab into the river. The place was not easily missed, though, with all the cars lined up alongside the road. That was the main attraction – parking— and a full moon, the name notwithstanding, was not a welcome guest.

There was at least one juke for Blacks that was run by a White man, but it was not very popular, perhaps for the following reason. Matt's daughter Nettie Mae remembered going there in 1949.

"This White guy ran this place; he had a juke box, beer and whiskey. Nobody had a license at this time to run a store, and Daddy let me go there one time with my cousin and his wife, the three of us. The owner told my cousin to bring me up there and the three of us go out. My cousin told him if he brings his cousin with him and the four of us could go out; he knew just what to say to put them in their place."

Attitudes toward women in Nelms County were chauvinistic—"boys will be boys"—and Matt transmitted these attitudes to his sons. For example, Matt would crack a hole in the top of a raw egg using the edge of a fork and pour a little salt and pepper on top of it and suck out the contents. When the girls were not around or turned up their noses and walked away, he would tell the boys in a subdued voice that sucking an egg would "put lead in your pencil." It was years before they understood what that meant. When they finally figured it out, they sucked a few eggs, but from their perspective, to extend the analogy, the problem was with paper, not pencil. Matt acquired this habit from Papa

Ed, who told him that it performed the same function as a mixture of herbs that grew only in Africa called "the bull" that was sold in the marketplace as an aphrodisiac. "The bull" was such a powerful potion that it was purchased with an antidote called "the bullock."

Chauvinism probably accounted for myths about sex among country boys. One myth was that masturbation caused blindness, but this myth was more pervasive in the city than the country. The most persistent belief was that a girl had a "sweet spot," frequently assumed to be in the palm of her hand, the back of her neck, or the nipple of her breast. All one had to do was locate and caress this spot to break down a young woman's resistance. When a boy kissed a girl, his hands were activated by this belief as he began running them over her body in search of that mythical "sweet spot." The place itself was elusive, but the consequences of the search were immediate and often painful.

Sexual attitudes could be cruel and ironic. Rufus Terry was hanging out with some boys who started giggling when Freddy Lewis "accidentally" mentioned that Rufus' girlfriend, Mamie Hargrove, was out with another boy. Everyone knew how much Rufus loved Mamie and how he thought she was a virgin even though she had a reputation of, in Freddy's words, "being a loose woman." Boys expected to marry virgins, but they were not held to this criterion. Girls were held to societal norms the way a dog was tethered to a tree. Rufus grabbed Freddy by the neck and started choking him for telling "lies" about Mamie. Clearer heads finally prevailed when Freddy admitted that he was "only joking." It was a risky business this double standard, since a young woman could hold out on the boy she expected to marry while giving in to the playboy who failed to meet her standards.

Of course, petting was as far as most dates went, since girls feared bad reputations almost as much as getting pregnant, and oral sex was considered a perversion by boys and girls. Some boys made up stories about their sexual exploits to put up a good front, but others were more innovative. After a baseball game one Saturday afternoon, players were celebrating their victory when James McNabb described in detail how he ejaculated into a rubber while grinding up against Jeannette Wilkes. Robert Brinson was so intrigued that he was determined to try this approach with his girlfriend Lucy Mae Nelson, but he first had to find a pack of condoms, the acquisition of which frequently required a reversal of racial neighborhoods.

The next night (Sunday) Bob arrived at Lucy Mae's house around 7:30 p.m. fully prepared for this experiment and soon convinced her to go along with his scheme. At a predetermined time, Bob would go to the bathroom, put on his rubber, and return to the living room where Lucy Mae would announce to her parents that they were going outside to the porch. Here they would neck until Bob accomplished his objective. About 8:30 p.m. they agreed to implement Bob's idea and he excused himself to the bathroom. He put his rubber on his erect penis and pointed it down his right leg to be as unobtrusive as possible as he walked back to the living room.

When Bob returned from the bathroom he unexpectedly found Lucy Mae's father, Joseph Nelson, sitting down on the sofa with her.

"Hi Bob, how are you?" Mr. Nelson asked.

"Um, fine," Bob said anxiously.

Mr. Nelson continued his conversation with Lucy Mae while Bob stood there with his hand in his pocket to hide his erection (every boy who has slow dragged on the dance floor had to become adept at this maneuver) instead of sitting down to bring less attention to himself. Perhaps he thought if he continued to stand up, Mr. Nelson would leave more quickly. At any rate, that did not happen. After a few minutes Bob's erection was rapidly slipping away and since he was not liberally endowed, the rubber began to slip off his penis. Bob wriggled his hand around to stop the condom from falling down his pants leg, but when he could not find it he began to panic. He thought, *What if the rubber falls out of my pants leg onto the floor?*

He decided to remain motionless, but Mr. Nelson, noticing that Bob was in some kind of pain, insisted that he sit down. Reluctantly, Bob dragged his right leg to the sofa, *leaving the rubber where he stood.* With all eyes, including his own, fixated on the spot where he stood, Bob bolted from the house, leaving Lucy Mae to face alone the full consequences of his experiment. He also left his father's car behind, giving no thought to the fact that he lived several miles away, but with full knowledge that no explanation in the world would save him from the wrath of Mr. Jo Jo Nelson.

Chapter 6

THE PERIPHERY OF THE PEDESTAL

In this so-called Negro race we
have the prettiest people in the
world. Why do we go away from
home to find what we already have
on hand!

Carter G. Woodson[5]

$\mathcal{M}$ att Nelms' store (the one he built after leaving the Big House) did not have a large sign out front that said "Matt Nelms' Groceries" or "Nelms' Grocery Store" or anything like that. But anyone passing by knew it was a business with a gas tank out front and advertisements on the building. The family just called it "the store." Bills that came in the mail said "Nelms' Groceries" or "Nelms' Grocery Store" Rural Delivery, Box 674. Neighbors called it "Matt's Store" and checker players called it "Matt's Place." By any name it was kind of like a social center for the people who lived in the Mt. Canaan area of the country.

The store was a few city blocks, maybe a tenth of a mile, down the hill from the house; traveling west on the main drag about twenty miles from the city of Tisdell, Georgia, nobody could miss it, especially at night when it was the only place around with a light and a car or two parked out front. The store was a frame building without windows, but there was a cut-out in the middle of the west wall with a swinging wooden gate, with leather hinges that opened like a window. The building had two distinct sections that varied slightly in size. The distinctiveness was a result of adding a new room to the older building to enlarge the store. The two structures wore their separate histories in a way that all could see who were willing to examine them closely beyond the red asbestos siding that overlapped both buildings in an unsuccessful attempt to conceal their unique identities.

Matt's store had a single entrance with a globe-less light overhead just above a large red and white Coca-Cola sign. As one faced the door, to the left there was a big rectangular Nehi sign with a very yellow background. Above the Nehi sign was a medium-sized Goody's sign that advertised Headache Powders (5 cents) and a smaller Kool sign that touted menthol cigarettes. To the right of the door was a Viceroy Filters sign with its bottom flipped up from the loss of its tacks; it invited patrons to "Come In." On the newer building farther to the right (east) was a large yellow, red, blue, and white Pepsi-Cola sign that was tacked on the wall where the older building and the addition came together; its purpose seemed to have been to deny the buildings their particularity.

As customers walked through the front door of the store, they had to step down to keep from tripping, as the concrete floor was about six inches below ground level. At night, the light above the door (left globe-less for more illumination) was a tremendous help. Directly in front of the entrance was a cash register, which showed the costs of purchases in a window that popped up when the keys were pushed. In the old store, cigar boxes—one for paper money and one for change—served that purpose. The cash register sat on about a four feet high wooden counter which held gum in a carton, a penny- operated bubble gum machine, boxes of candy, Lays potato chips and pig skins on a rack, and Lance crackers in a jar. Pickled pigs' feet and sausage were also on the counter in a jar. The shelves contained all kinds of canned goods including sardines, Vienna sausages, pork-and-beans, canned oysters, Carnation milk and so on. To the left of the counter were drink and ice cream boxes. There were few dry goods. Drink-bottle crates were lined all around the wall which people used for seats, mostly during checker games or discussions. The interior walls of the store had different kinds of signs, including a clock that advertised various products; some even lit up or had flashing lights.

Matt sold gas, which his children pumped for the customers; there was no self- service. At one time he sold Shell or Texaco (Sky Chief with an elongated glass where the gas could be seen), but Sinclair gasoline (with a green dinosaur on the tank) was sold most often. Trucks delivered the goods from wholesalers in Tisdell, but Matt bought most of his trinkets, dry goods, medicinal or non-edible items from a traveling salesman called Mr. Stocks, an appropriate name for a stocky White man. He was well liked by the Black people who knew him. He had a son, called Whitey, maybe a year older than the twins. Whitey was a spoiled kid, but not a spoiled-acting kid. He had BB guns, toy cars, firecrackers, small knives, baseball cards and a bike that Mr. Stocks carried on top of his Pontiac station wagon. The back seat of the car had been removed to provide more room for his goods. Whitey wasn't selfish about any of his things; that's why he was not considered spoiled-acting. He even got the boys in the neighborhood to buy toy telegraph sets from Mr. Stocks and learn the Morse code.

Mr. Stocks did not have that air of superiority that most White men had, even though he was an obvious southerner with a deep southern drawl. Mr. Stocks told Matt that he had been raised by a Colored woman, though it was not exactly clear what that meant, since many racist White men were raised by Black women. Perhaps that explained, at least to him, why he didn't demand the conformity to racial etiquette that White men seemed to think was as important as the air they breathed. He used to tell Matt to call him Stocks, not "Mr. Stocks," but Matt never did.

Deep down inside, Matt didn't trust White people and would never have put himself in a position that they could turn on him for violating some racial code.

Matt carried a line of goods he got from Mr. Stocks that included cigarettes, cigars, batteries, knives, flashlights, medicines or ointments/ liniments (castor oil, cod liver oil, Three Sixes, iodine, and black draught or "black draw" as some called it). Outside one could find turnips, cabbage, potatoes, peas, corn, and other items raised by the family from the farm. Those perishable items that didn't sell quickly found their way into Rena's pots. Matt also carried a few dry goods or clothes, like socks and long cotton drawers (LCDs) acquired from Mr. Stocks. Some farm products like fertilizers, seeds, hoes, and shovels could also be bought at Matt's store, but he didn't always keep such things in stock. There was also a supply of pesticides like fly spray that had to be put in a device with a cylinder and handle which, when pushed, sprayed the insect killer on the same principle as the pop guns the boys made. The spray had a bad odor, but it did not last long and was much more tolerable than the unhealthy-looking fly paper Matt had strung all around the store. The flies banged into the paper and struggled helplessly for what seemed like hours to hang on to dear life.

Matt owned most of the land around the immediate area of his store in every direction, except that which he sold to members of the church, his son Kalem, his brothers Jake and Walton, and other Black people. You might say this allowed him to control the character of the community. Mr. Stocks was the only White man he sold an acre of land to, about a quarter mile from his store eastward toward Tisdell. This was about the same time that Mr. Stocks talked Matt into putting in a juke box and pinball and slot machines. Mr. Stocks kept the key to the money boxes of these devices, but Matt had a key to get inside to repair them. For example, when the record stuck on the juke box Matt could open it up to correct the problem. Stocks came about once a month to get the money out of these machines which was split 50-50 with Matt. It was not long before the sheriff came and took the slot machines away even though he did not arrest Matt.

When Stocks moved a trailer onto the property he bought from Matt and decided to live there with a woman, his son Whitey, and another man in the middle of the Black community, Matt regretted that he sold that land to a White man, "even Mr. Stocks," as he put it. More disheartening and somewhat insulting was that Stocks built a little shack beside the trailer and sold those items that Matt ordinarily bought from him to resell, an act that reinforced his belief that you could not trust White folks. Matt's cow dung philosophy personified, he continued to do some business with Mr. Stocks, albeit under strained conditions.

Matt allowed his children to run the store, and most of them got a reputation for being smart. Matt and Rena taught all their kids to read, write, and count at an early age. Rena focused on school work while Matt paid more attention to their out-of-school education. It was not that Matt valued education less than his wife; his interest came from a practical standpoint, since he expected his children to run his store without giving away his money or his goods. He also expected his children to follow in his footsteps and go into a business of their own, the reason he tolerated their operating mini-businesses with goods from his store.

Matt used to make his kids count backwards from and forwards to a hundred until they could do it with equal facility. He thought that counting backwards made them better at calculations. He also used to give them exercises to work out by calculating the change to be given to a customer in a specific situation. He would, for example, take a cinnamon roll and a pack of tobacco off the shelf and take out a dollar bill and ask them to tell him how much change he was due. He would get two Cokes from the drink box and a can of oysters and ask how much he owed. Sometimes he took several items that cost more than he gave them and expected them to ask for the rest of the money. When teaching the children how to count, Matt used to say if a customer came into the store and got the notion to buy a can of sardines and a box of saltine crackers and gave you a five- dollar bill, how much change do you owe him? The children would do the computations and give an answer, but the correct response was "no change" because the customer had not bought anything, he only got the "notion" to buy. All such exercises had to be done in the head, no paper or pencil could be used, and the children competed to see who would be first to come up with the right answer. The children proudly showed off their arithmetic skills in front of strangers.

Whites and Blacks generally stayed in different parts of the county, but their activities inevitably brought them into contact. Matt, Rena, and another couple were out driving one Sunday afternoon and were confronted by some Whites out doing the same thing—except they were drinking. They stopped Matt—all Whites in those days had police power over all Blacks—and asked him some questions about where they were going. Matt answered to avoid trouble, and they told Matt and his companions to go on. Resistance was clearly the wrong thing to do, as these people started shooting pistols as soon as they left, and one of the women was heard shouting, "shoot your pistol, daddy."

Matt's regular customers were Blacks who lived in the neighborhood—checker players, long-time acquaintances and his employees. He extended credit to neighbors and friends who needed to get by until the next check, and sometimes people owed him money that was never paid. Infrequent customers included Black and White passersby traveling to and from Tisdell, a few Whites who preferred to purchase certain items away from their neighborhood, and occasional troublemakers who made the store a racial testing ground. One White couple had the habit of stopping to chat without buying anything. Every time they came, Miss Bonnie wanted water and they all—Miss Bonnie, her husband, and two children—drank from the same dipper as Matt's family, but Miss Bonnie had snuff running from the side of her mouth when she used the family's dipper.

Rena told the children she didn't want Miss Bonnie drinking from the dipper, so the next time they came, young Hattie told her, "Miss Bonnie, my mama said you can't drink out of us dipper cause you keep your mouth too nasty." Hattie added the last part on her own.

Rena didn't know how to tell this White woman, and had told the children to hide the dipper and when they saw her to give her a cup, but Hattie told her anyway.

There was the time when a White man came into Matt's store and struck up a conversation about how fast his car was. He was no stranger; he had been in the store before, but he lived in Johnson County about twenty-five miles away due west, but on the same road as Matt's store. He drove one of those Studebakers, with a bullet nose in the grille, that looked like a small airplane. This was sometimes in the late 1950s. The man indicated that he left home when the program he had been watching on television was going off and that he had arrived at Matt's store just about the time he thought the next program had begun. Since there was no television in the store, the man used the Coca-Cola clock in the store to make the point.

According to what he heard, Lonnie calculated that the man must be mistaken. He thought, *how on earth could this man travel twenty-five miles in less than five minutes?*

Anxious to show Matt his expertise at calculations, Lonnie looked up at the man and started to say, "Mister, you are —"

It was not clear whether Lonnie was going to say "lying" or "mistaken," but either way, the words never came out of his mouth because Matt whacked him hard across the face. "Shut up, boy!" Matt had already figured out that this wasn't possible, but chose not to contradict the man.

Lonnie had two lessons graphically reinforced by his father's reaction. First, young people did not enter the conversations of adults, a lesson they learned at an early age and often at a prime price. Second, and, more significantly, Lonnie learned he must not breach racial etiquette, the code of behaviors that regulated interactions between Blacks and Whites. No Black person, certainly not a boy, called a White man a liar in the 1950s, regardless of the veracity of the man's remarks. Anxious to show his father how smart he was, something a White child could do with impunity, Lonnie had a lapse in judgment.

Some White customers came to the store to purchase items they did not want to buy in their neighborhood. Young White boys, some of today's substantial citizens in Nelms County, came to Matt's store to buy cigarettes and chewing tobacco. Matt did not sell alcohol, nor did Kalem, to teenagers.

"Matt, you got any rubbers?" a White boy yelled from the window of his car.

The question was asked well within the hearing of all those in the store and without shame or embarrassment. You can only guess that the young girl who sat so close to him one could hardly tell there were two people in the car already understood that she was not merely out for an evening ride. For these teenage boys to buy these items in White-owned stores ran the risk of exposing their intentions to other Whites, so they came to Matt's store. They had no reason to be embarrassed in front of Black people; embarrassment was a function of equality. The transaction did contribute to the rumor that young White men came to Miss Pleutsy to "take care" of their pregnant girlfriends, but nobody knew for sure. Miss Pleutsy was a respected midwife and an alleged conjure woman, but nobody knew for certain about all her business.

Some Whites learned that the boundaries of racial etiquette were less expansive in Matt's store than elsewhere. There was this time when a White man who had been in the store a couple times came in and stood by the counter. He knew nothing about Matt, except that he looked like any other White man who operated a country store. On this day, Andrew was behind the counter dusting and straightening the canned goods on the shelves.

The White man leaned over the counter to Matt and whispered, "you see that little nigger boy there? you better watch him, I can tell you, he will steal."

Matt looked around for some strange boy, but all he saw was Andrew.

"You mean that boy there?" Matt asked.

"Yeah," he replied.

"Anything in this store already belongs to him. He don't have to steal; that boy is my son." Matt said.

"You a nigra?" the man asked as he started to the door. "Nigra" was a bastardized form of Negro that Whites used, but Black people found it as offensive as "nigger."

On another afternoon, Elouise was keeping store and Kalem was running the automobile repair shop next door when a Caucasian man stopped, went over to the drink box, got a Pepsi, and drank it. He was leaving without paying and Elouise ran next door and told Kalem, who came out and told him to pay up. He said Elouise had picked his pocket and taken his wallet. Kalem told him she was his sister and didn't pick pockets. Evidently he responded with something that angered Kalem, because the next thing Elouise knew he had his rifle in his hand and was telling the man to get in his car and leave and not stop there anymore. When he passed going back up the road, he was zooming past, according to Elouise.

Matt tried to protect his daughters from undesirable suitors and situations, but it didn't always work. Nellie Mae got married at age fourteen and Matt's objections fell on deaf ears since he and Rena were married at that age. Elouise was pregnant and married at sixteen, unfortunately in that order, but no "shotgun" was necessary. Matt particularly tried to protect his daughters from White men who used the protection of White women as a ruse to deny basic rights to Black men. Matt didn't want them doing domestic work, but reluctantly made exceptions, allowing them to babysit in the evenings and work part time during the summer when school was not in session. When incidents occurred, Rena and the girls conspired unsuccessfully to conceal them from their father.

Catherine, for example, was permitted to work two days a week for a well-known Nelms County lawyer. One Sunday when his wife was away, he requested Catherine because he was having company and needed someone to cook and serve the guests. Catherine recalled:

"When I arrived, he [the lawyer] had planned to do something else—he wanted me to be his mistress. He said he would give me a hundred dollars a week and I told him I did not mix and he said I was already mixed so I told him that was my grandmother's doing, not mine, so he paid me for that day and I did not go back to work for him after that."

Another incident involved Teresa, who was employed part time for another prominent family. The man came home from work in the afternoon and tried to rape her. She escaped, walked home, and explained what happened to her mother with no intention of telling her father. Matt found out anyway and went after the man with his shotgun. Matt was on his way to the man's house when he cooled down and decided to discuss the issue with Mr. Kin Lamb, who promised he would take care of it and convinced Matt to return home. How Mr. Kin handled it is unknown.

Another incident involving Teresa several years later was more ominous.

"That daughter Teresa sure pretty, Matt," said Richard Pratt, a White customer.

Pratt had recently moved to the country from some part of Alabama, having lived in the area only a few months. He had only been in the store once before, but it was one of the peculiarities of the South that White people were like elephants when it came to a Black person's first name, but developed amnesia about last names. Maybe it had something to do with the fact that they all had the same first name: "Mister." When Pratt made the comment everyone in the store became tensely silent. Those playing checkers had already turned their attention away from the game, as they were wont to do when a White man came into the store.

"My daughter is not your concern. She here to work and you here to buy. Best we get on with our business, and if you don't have any business, it's best you just get on." Matt said this without any expectation of a rebuttal.

The red in Pratt's face indicated that he understood but was bitter. To him, Matt had crossed the line; no Black man had the right to talk that way to a White man, the subject notwithstanding. Pratt left tail-tucked, but there was no laughter afterwards, because Matt considered the encounter more dangerous than funny. Those who witnessed the incident merely returned to what they were doing.

Several weeks passed before this incident was brought to closure. One day, Matt was in Helgarten's General Merchandise Store about five miles down the road from his store. Matt purchased equipment like plows, saws, wire and seed from old man Helgarten, who sometimes extended him credit to operate when he needed it. On this occasion Richard Pratt was in Helgarten's store when Matt arrived. He had been stewing over the incident at Matt's store and waiting for an opportunity to get back at Matt for his insult. It was rather common knowledge that Matt himself had an eye for women and on occasion had done more than cast a fleeting eye.

When an attractive, middle-aged White woman walked into Helgarten's store to pay for the gas that Helgarten's "retarded" son Louis had pumped for her, Pratt said, "Matt, **SHE** looks good to you, don't she?"

Matt tried to ignore him. The woman, not knowing what to make of this, looked at Matt, glanced back at Pratt, dropped her money on the counter, and hurried from the store. She obviously smelled trouble and wanted no part of it.

"Matt, she looks good to you, don't she," Pratt repeated, well within the hearing of Hellgarten and the other two white men in the store.

These men knew Matt better than this newcomer and maybe one of them wished they could help rescue Matt from this difficult situation, but racial convention demanded their silence. White men all over the Jim Crow South would do anything for a Black "friend"—bail him out of jail, lend him money, intervene with the law—but would not lift a finger to change an unjust system.

Matt was on the horns of the bull. He realized that to say the woman did not look good would be taken as an insult to her, which was certain to bring another response from the bigoted Pratt. On the other hand, to say that she was attractive would indicate that he desired what he saw, an even greater transgression of racial etiquette. Matt wanted to say that the woman was not his business, which was what he had told Pratt about his daughter, but he didn't feel that would make the point. He decided that the lesser of two evils was to say that she didn't look good.

"She looks like shit to me," Matt replied.

This comment brought the kind of silence to the place that one finds when the White sheriff walks into a room of Black people. It seemed for a minute that even the mice that played in Helgarten's hay loft stood still, and his mentally challenged son, Louis, who was always swaying and moving back and forth, stood dead still for the first time. Matt did not wait for a rebuttal. He said, "I can get women as White as her, and as pretty, if she is pretty to you, and *I don't have to leave my own race*; we got all colors in my race—black, brown, and even as fair as that lady. You have to leave your race to go into another community to find any other color, which I don't have to do. I can stick with my people and get any color I want within my race," Matt explained.

One of the men in the store said, "he got you there!"

Matt believed these men accepted his explanation. Old man Helgarten, who had done business with Matt for over twenty years, was pleased with Matt's maneuver, even if he did not know what to make of his initial response. Helgarten followed him outside, all the time warning him to keep an eye on that "po white trash," a phrase Matt never used.

Matt got away with an unsavory comment about a White woman. Few men could have pulled off such a stunt. Matt did not want Pratt to return to his store expecting to be treated differently than before. He believed that saying the woman looked like shit would be overlooked if it were connected to a more cherished racial code—that is, he desired only women of his own race.

Chapter 7

WHO KNOWS MY NAME?

As a man name is so is he.

> 1 Samuel 25:25

Your name will live when you
have died.

> Swahili Proverb[6]

*S*ome country people discovered when they got older that their birth certificates, filled out by Miss Hilda or Miss Pleusty, had misspelled names or the wrong names altogether. Men named James were "Jones," Frank became "Fank," women named Virginia were "Vagina," and the last name Nelms was sometimes spelled "Nims." When these people tried to "correct" these errors at the probate office, they faced some insensitive White woman who insisted they were changing the names they had lived with for forty or fifty years. They were then told that they needed certain items to make the "change" – marriage licenses, school attendance records, drivers' licenses, baptismal records, old bills, Bibles and so on – but when they showed up with these things, they were not enough. Black folks who objected to this treatment were considered "uppity" and were told they needed an appointment to complete the process. Discouraged, some people took their problems to the state capital in Atlanta, where officials understood that midwives were not always educated and names have histories and traditions.

Many country people used nicknames so often that even friends didn't always know each other's real names. When one of these individuals died and the real name was published in the newspaper without the nickname, it was months before people realized the person had passed on. Some of these informal names seemed peculiar or unusual, but their origin was not random. There was a "P.J." for Peter Jones, a "J.C." for Jackie Carter, and there were two Richards, Richard Moore and Richard Coleman. The former was called "R.M." and the latter was called "R.C." like the drink. Obviously, the first initials accounted for these nicknames. There were no "Dicks" among the Richards. Whatever cultural or linguistic process Whites used to convert Richard to Dick did not work in the country. Sometimes the first name was shortened, like "Ray" for "Raymond" or the last part of a name, like "Velt" for "Listervelt" could make a nickname. Girls were not given nicknames as generously as boys, but they had variations of their names like "Deb" for "Deborah" or "Barb" for "Barbara."

Sometimes Black folks got nicknames because of something they had done, the way they looked, or something about their personality. There was a guy called "Pretty Cap" because he had a habit of wearing caps he thought made him look good. There was a man called "Joe College" who had a habit of dropping a big word on you in conversation. There was a guy called "Slightly" who walked so lightly he just glided across the ground, and another man dubbed "Walking Walter" whom you could leave at one place and before you drove to the next place he was there, even though he never owned a car. There was a "Smokey," but the origin of his name is unknown except he had a father called "Cigar," which may offer some hint. There was a "Deek," short for Deacon who entertained his friends by pretending to preach. No one knows why he wasn't called "Preacher." There was also "Praying Ben," a deacon at Mt. Canaan Church who prayed so long about thirty folks had gathered outside the door waiting for him to finish praying.

No one liked being called out of their names, but this did

not stop some employers or acquaintances from using names that Blacks themselves did not use. Whites rarely concerned themselves with Black folks' last names and wrongly assumed that every Robert was "Bob," every William was "Bill," and every Anthony was "Tony." Sometimes they even used names that were hateful or stereotypical. Steve Burton, a newcomer to the country, said he was stamped with the name "Coon" by the White man he worked for in Elberton County, and he even used the name himself. Paul Wright was called "Nig," but the origin of his nickname is unknown except his older brother had a habit of calling him "my Nigger," which he thought was affectionate. Country folks never used these names without surnames. They always said "Nig Wright" or "Coon Burton." Perhaps they thought using both names mitigated the insult.

Matt's girls had "boyfriends" with nicknames they sometimes assigned to themselves. A guy named Luke Carr liked to call himself "Hanger" because he says that he hung bigger than anyone else. "Skeeter" was so named because he gained a reputation as a young boy for skeeting pee ten to twelve feet longer than his nearest rival. He joked that he was successful because he had a longer barrel than the other boys. Ironically, Skeeter claimed he lost his title to Lucy Youman or "Skeeting Youman" because, as he put it, Lucy was using a double barrel.

Occasionally a physical characteristic provided an informal name for a person. "Chubby" was a name for young fat boys, and "Bull" was for a big, muscular guy. There was a guy called "Jack Booty" who was a short fellow whose butt was so high he had no waistline. An accident or disease could also nickname a person. A man named "Nubby" was called that because he lost two fingers at the sawmill Matt once owned. There were several people called "Foots" and "Feet" for obvious reasons. There was "Bad Foot" Jenkins who should really have been called "Bad Toe," since he used to cut up all his shoes so that his big toe would be unmolested by the touch of leather. They say he had "gouch," which one can only assume meant gout. "Bad Foot" used to say that when he had a bout of "gouch" his foot hurt so badly he slept in the dark because he didn't want the light to hit it.

Sometimes a physical characteristic would be reversed to make a nickname— Rena's mother, who was dark skinned, was called "Snow." There was also this huge woman who used to come into Matt's store who said, when asked her name, "Just call me Tiny." Names not only reflected personality, but could predetermine it. Joe was a name for a person who almost universally fathomed himself a lover or Casanova and Ray was always a congenial fellow whom everybody liked. When these names were doubled, the personality was reversed. For example, "Jo Jo" was a bully who liked to throw his weight around. The same was true of Ray when changed to "Ray Ray" who became a mean character. Of course, this doubling worked only for males, since there was no discernible difference between Dee and "Dee Dee" or Lue and a "LuLu."

What happened to Amanda Richards, called "Teary" is the best example of a tragedy naming a person. Amanda was a very beautiful young woman with "good features" and green eyes that were the source of limitless speculation. Boys constantly told Amanda how pretty she was, the family bragged on her beauty, and girls conceded her attractiveness. She made good grades in school and teachers said Amanda was very bright, but she valued her good looks above her intelligence. All these praises led Amanda to laud her good looks over those with large noses, dark skin, or kinky hair—features she saw as unattractive. She refused to listen when old people told her that no good comes of vanity and reminded her that Rev. Whatley had preached many sermons claiming that "a proud look" was at the top of the things God hated most.

One night, Amanda's family home caught fire and burned completely to the ground. The fire evidently started in the hearth around the fireplace, since some children said there was a loud "pop" late that night, which was believed to be a fireball that sometimes pops out of the fireplace. The family was asleep until awakened by a neighbor who saw the fire from a distance. When the family was roused, they discovered that the doorway from the children's bedrooms was blocked by fire, but they managed to get them all out from the windows except Amanda, who slept in the bed closest to the wall where the fire had started. By the time she was pulled from the blaze she was burned badly, her beautiful face disfigured. The disaster burned away her lower eyelid and she looked like someone had pulled the lower skin from around her eye to locate some foreign object. Her left eye constantly drained and appeared that she was always in tears.

It was no surprise to elderly people who had warned her that God punished the vain, but those less inclined to religious explanation thought this was going too far. After the incident, Amanda became a devout Christian, ever ready to do good deeds in the community, proving once again to believers that God worked in mysterious ways. Wherever you found pain, death, or distress there was "Miss Teary." She married a preacher over in Oglethorpe County and they started a new church—the Benevolent Baptist Mission—which was devoted to charitable activities. Amanda was soon thought of as a saint – one of the redeemed.

Although these nicknames might have seemed strange to outsiders, conformity ruled in the country. People considered "deviants" were virtually nonexistent. The only drug people used was moonshine; marijuana and other drugs were essentially unheard of. People didn't speak openly about homosexuality and boys applied the term "sissy" to almost any boy considered weak or who behaved differently. There *were* these two women who attended Mt. Canaan Missionary Baptist Church that people whispered about. People said they were too close to have a "natural" relationship. The rumor mill held that they were something called "bull daggers." In a place where the bull symbolized virility and manhood these "b-u-l-l-daggers" must have posed quite an irony.

Another unmentionable thing was incest, but again there was this exception. There was a house on the same dirt road where Matt lived with his first wife that was always closed and nobody ever saw anyone outside. The only signs of life were this pickup truck parked outside the house, which was not always in the same spot, and the smoke from the chimney in the winter time that gave evidence of human presence. When Matt's children got older, they learned that a man had lived there with two families—they never heard the name mentioned. Perhaps people thought that to speak their name condoned their lifestyle. The man who lived there had married a woman who had several children by previous marriages and liaisons, including a grown daughter, and he had two or three children of his own from a former marriage. He became involved with his step daughter and had several children by her. Apparently, children of incest just look like everybody else, since no one recognized them.

There was one very memorable character in the country considered by most people to be the only real deviant in the Mt. Canaan community. He used to sit outside Matt's store and talk to himself the whole time he was there, which was sometimes all day. He looked like he had never had a bath or a shave and smelled bad. His clothes, a matching pair of pants and coat—a suit—with a white shirt, were unkempt and rarely changed, though they looked like they had been expensive at one time. His shirt was long-sleeved and buttoned right up to the neck even in the summer when it was a hundred degrees. He did not wear but carried a tie that hung out of his coat pocket like he had just returned from some formal affair. He had a long, unkempt beard, un-brushed yellow teeth, and knotty, uncut hair which looked like the snakes of Medusa. Matt used to make him leave the store, because customers who didn't know him drove away when they saw him in front of the store talking to himself; Matt didn't mind so much when he chose not to leave but to go around to the side or back of the store.

His name was Bussey Newton, but the children called him "Combat" because he always seemed at war with himself, making gestures with his hands that acted out what he was saying—crouching, ducking, swinging his arms and fists like he was in a boxing match. He seemed to be flailing at some demons trying to attack him all the time. Some people claimed members of his family were cursed with dementia or senility (not words they used), and the trauma of catching his wife in bed with another man triggered what was always there—in the genes, they said. Other people said his wife put roots on him after he tried to kill her. He did manage to kill the man he caught in bed with her by hacking him to pieces with a knife. After that, his wife was afraid of him and refused to live with him. Black men in those days hardly went to jail for killing another Black man, but killing one in his own house, in his own bed, with his own wife, almost earned him a medal. Even the religious community accepted the consequences for getting caught sleeping with another man's wife. Since Black men could not punish Whites for doing it, it seemed that they were especially cruel to one another for such behavior.

Newton's talking sounded like gibberish; even when you listened closely you could only make out a word here and there. For several days Lonnie, Ronnie, and a group of boys from the neighborhood listened to Combat from around the corner of Matt's store. Each one jotted down the words that he could make out and Velt, who didn't ordinarily take part in mean schemes, pieced them together to come up with some of what Combat was saying:

> Makin' um luv, fuking whilst um woking. Don' makin' luv me lak dat noway, dese luv sounds, no make none soun' fer me. Didn' say shit did it, wid

him makin' all dese souns moans um goans, had kill him, ned to kill em both. Had damn die, not me none, me no souns. Wok day long som to eat, what you wok for and sit up roun yo house, serve to die and do again kill em both I coul. Didn' mak nos soun fer me no, no but fer him gotta damn die, no good snake, no souns fer me. Fukin whilst um wokin, that fair, no sirree, fukin whilst um wokin, huh fukin whilst um wokin.

For weeks, the kids would run up to Combat and say, "fukin while um woking" or "make no sound for me," and when he started after them they ran like crazy so that he could not catch them. After a week or so, Matt discovered what they had done and made them stop teasing him. Matt was afraid that Combat would hurt one of them even though he seemed harmless enough. Sometime after that when Matt was alone, he found himself mumbling,"fuking whilst um woking, fuking whilst um woking, and shaking his head, "my, my, my."

Chapter 8

MY BROTHER'S KEEPER

We in the South love the Negro in his
place - but his place is at the back door
with his hat in his hand.
Eugene Talmadge, Governor of Georgia[7]

*D*uring the Jim Crow era, Blacks exercised no political power er in Nelms County, even though there were only slightly more Whites than Blacks. That's the way it had been for as long as most folks could remember. Some old people did talk about Blacks voting after emancipation. At that time, called Reconstruction, at least one African- American from Nelms County, a man named Elijah Morgan, made it all the way to the Georgia state legislature, where he and his Black colleagues were kicked out. By the time the US Congress reinstated them, Morgan and his family had fled to California to escape the threats of the local Ku Klux Klan.

When the city of Tisdell began desegregating in the late 1950s, Whites fled to Nelms County to escape what they called "forced integration" and began a process that made the county overwhelmingly White. Soon afterwards, the county itself had to desegregate and the school board stripped the names of Black schools, even those named for Whites, to accommodate segregationists who did not want their children attending former Black schools. A little later, a new breed of political leaders began naming bridges, buildings, and roads for White men (no women), some of whom had never set foot in Nelms County. A few Black men got their names on back roads and alleys where Whites didn't drive on them on a regular basis. Elijah Morgan was not among them. Neither was Matt Nelms, perhaps because the White Nelms family already dominated enough things. Eventually, Black communities were given names, none of which reflected the oral traditions of the Black population. "Sweetwater" was chosen for the Mt. Canaan Community, where the Nelms family called the country. The name left a sour taste in the mouths of the old residents and eroded their sense of belonging.

The normal avenues to power closed to them, African-Americans exercised only informal power derived from their relationship to a "good-ole-boy-system." In addition, the traditional source of leadership from the Black church was limited because most pastors lived outside Nelms County. Blacks who did have influence fell into two categories. They were either opportunists willing to play out any fiction that Whites created, or pragmatists who cooperated with Whites to help their people. Blacks owed their civil rights to neither group, but to protests from places like Tisdell, where students at the Black college helped alter race relations. Generally, Whites and Blacks had gotten along well during the era of Jim Crow, no doubt due more to the fact that Blacks understood their place rather than harmonious relations between equals.

The wealthy White families like the Nelms, Lambs, McNeils, and Bransfords were the power brokers who served as the school superintendents, county clerks, probate judges, and members of the Board of Education and County Commission. The Branfords and Lambs were well liked and Matt considered Kindred Lamb, from whom he had rented the Big House and sometimes borrowed money, a trusted friend. Whenever Matt and the children went to "Mr. Kin's" house, the children had the run of the place, unlike other places where Matt made them stay in the truck. The children rode the Lambs' horses, took pecans from the orchards, and played with Mr. Kin's grandchildren.

The most vivid memory the children had of going to Mr. Kin's house was when Matt went there to "cut his hogs," that is, to remove their testicles; he never used the word "castrate." Matt also brought them home to cook, but somewhere between the cutting and the bringing, they were transformed into something called "mountain oysters." Rena did the cooking, but she drew the line here; she would neither cook nor eat hog "nuts," despite their metamorphosis into a kind of seafood. Matt cooked them himself and the children ate them as well. Their best recollection was that they were tastier than the fried hog brains and eggs Matt had for breakfast.

Among the Blacks who had influence with the Whites, no one outdistanced Kalem Nelms, who was one of two children Matt fathered between marriages that led Gama Staten to call him "the ole baby maker." Kalem was reared by his mother and maternal grandparents, whose last name was Rossiter. When his mother married, Kalem remained with his grandparents, who died a few months apart when he was about eighteen years of age. That same year he met and married Irene Ramsey, bought land from Matt, and changed his name from Kalem Rossiter to Kalem Nelms. They had three children, Kalem Jr. or Lil Kal, Marlene, and Henry, called Hank. He built a house and garage across the street from Matt and Rena. It is not altogether clear why he made this decision, but he evidently forgave Matt's transgression and chose to claim what was rightfully his—the Nelms name. Kalem became a big brother who helped to look after his siblings, especially the twins. Biologically he might have been a half-brother, but it was sociology that mattered growing up country.

When Elizabeth heard what Kalem had done, she included in one of her letters the following:

"If I was Kalem I would not want to be near you after you got my mother pregnant and didn't marry her."

Elizabeth was the only one who could have said this to Matt, but Rena objected to her "insulting" remarks and told her so. Elizabeth, as one who held sacred the belief that "the truth shall set you free," was not one to regret saying it. Matt had his feelings hurt. Perhaps he realized Kalem was more like him than many of his children by Rena.

Kalem and Matt exerted influence in the community because of their success in business and willingness to help others. While Matt was a church leader, Kalem's power base was drawn from his relationship with important White people, especially the sheriff, Herbert Cranford. The sheriff was not from one of the wealthy White families, but he was the most powerful person in the county when it came to Black folks. He and his father Nelson Cranford before him had held the sheriff's office in Nelms County for more than four decades, from the 1920s to the 1960s, though neither of them had a very good reputation among Black folks. But Kalem was an unofficial "deputy" and even carried a gun most of the time. When court was held in the county seat, it attracted people to Drayton from many different places. Kalem, a talented cook, spent the entire time (sometimes several weeks) barbecuing hogs, goats, and chickens and making hash and sauces to feed the hungry judges, lawyers, and businessmen who came to the courthouse. Kalem blended into the environment (Black people are said to be invisible anyway), and listened to these people talk about the federal government, politics, and race to learn as much as he could. He also got to know personally many important people at a time when a White supporter was the only chance a Black man had in the White man's court.

Deference to White people was commonplace for Black people, but the tactic should not be confused with the person. Kalem stood up for his rights at the risk of personal harm and was no "Uncle Tom," despite what the misinformed might have observed. He fixed a White man's car one time and the man came to pick it up without the money. When Kalem refused to give him the car, the man threatened him. Kalem put his gun in his face and sent him away on foot. With the influence Kalem exerted because of his relationship with law enforcement, he could get a ticket torn up with a simple request, get a drunk out of jail with a phone call, and could go on a bond with a simple "Yes sir, I will stand for it." Those most likely to blame him for "wearing the mask" were the first to call when a son or grandson ran afoul of the law.

Matt sold his store to Kalem and built a new one made of concrete blocks farther down the road on the opposite side. Kalem now operated a garage, a store, and a juke joint all next door to one another. His garage had these wide doors and cement floor but with open rafters used to hang pulleys and chains to pull engines from cars. Kalem's juke joint was built next to the garage and they shared the west wall. The juke was made of wood with red asbestos siding. It had two rooms—or three, depending on your perspective. There was one long room about forty feet that extended most of the length of the garage, with a partition that separated the dance floor from the pool hall. It had a smaller room off to the right as you entered the front door that served as a kitchen where customers could walk up to the counter and buy sausages, hot dogs, fish sandwiches, and drinks. Moonshine (a name it got because it was made by the light of the moon, called "scrap iron" or "shine" by country people) could be had, but its purchase required a clandestine transaction wherever it was sold in a "dry county."

Kalem had a gentle character, even though he could be tough when necessary. He smoked a pack of Camels cigarettes and put away about a fifth of whiskey a day, but not a single person in the county could swear he ever saw him drunk. Kalem was compassionate and generous (he would literally give you the shirt off his back), and honest, (no one ever accused him of overcharging them for auto repairs).

He also had a great sense of humor. When he was told that he was getting old, he said, "I may be too old to cut the mustard, but I can always lick the jar."

When he was told he was getting fat, he responded, "it's a poor mechanic who doesn't build a shed over his tools."

A good example of these qualities is illustrated by a story about Frances Whatley, the daughter of Mt. Canaan's pastor. She had car trouble and managed to get her automobile to Kalem's shop before it died on her. It limped up to the front of the garage with smoke coming from under the hood and making a lot of rattling noise. Frances thought her car was on fire and asked Kalem to check it while she sat down in the store to catch her breath. He took about thirty minutes before he came in to give her the bad news.

"Ma'am, you got a lot of problems. Your car's William Pen flew loose from the wobbling shafts, tore into the penium gear and ruptured the acceleration compressor. As if that wasn't bad enough, ma'am, the left differential broke the right differential and caused the fraction bar to release the steering chassis, striking the oil chamber and releasing the vapor locks."

By this time, Frances Whatley was sobbing uncontrollably. "What am I going to do? I can't buy another car. How can I get home—what am I going to do?"

She was so distraught that Kalem, who had planned to have a lot more fun with her, had to quickly tell her he was just kidding. He explained that the car had run hot and probably needed a $2 thermostat and some antifreeze; both could be replaced for about $15. She then realized it was a joke and regained her composure.

Matt and Kalem were friends as well as father and son, but there was one thing that set them apart: Kalem was not a member of the church. Kalem was said to be influenced by his mother's Cherokee heritage and turned off by the hypocrisy of churchgoers, though he never accused Matt of this flaw. Besides, he said it was unnecessary for him to go church because **church came**

to him. After services on Sundays, many men came to the back door of Kalem's pool hall to continue satisfying their appetite for whiskey, which was, if you will forgive the sacrilege, triggered by a taste of communion wine.

As a courtesy, the revenue men always called the local sheriff before a night raid on moonshiners. He would then warn those he protected like Kalem who moved the "still" (distillery) before they arrived. At the time he was caught, the "revenoors" suspected collusion and conveniently "forgot" to tell the sheriff until after they caught Kalem with his still going full blast. Kalem went to jail for a few days, primarily because he refused to name any partners he might have had. Under Lil Kal's direction, the flow of alcohol was unabated. It is part of southern folklore about fast cars transporting moonshine, and Junior fit right in this tradition. Chevrolet didn't make a V-8 until 1955, but Lil Kal, who had learned mechanics from his father, had a '54 Chevy with a V-8 from a 1956 Pontiac, a retrofitting that required setting the radiator almost in the grille. It had an automatic in the floor that he shifted like a four-speed with each gear capable of burning rubber. The car made him one of the most popular boys in high school.

Lonnie and Ronnie were the first of Matt's and Rena's children to graduate from college, but Listervelt was the first in the Nelms family. The work ethic they acquired growing up country paid off because they worked their way through college with jobs at furniture stores, lumber companies, gas stations, construction jobs, and even an ice-making company. When Lonnie was a freshman, he worked at a grocery store/gas station about a mile from home. The owner of the store was a White man with two last names, Rogers Burgess. He had two high school daughters about a year apart who liked to help Lonnie pump gas and check oil and developed a habit of studying outside with him. A member of the Ku Klux Klan sent Kalem a message to tell his brother to stay away from the Burgess girls.

About a year later, Kalem got Lonnie a job helping him and some other men build the foundation for a dairy for a cousin of the sheriff's named Leonard Cranford. One day this man came out of his makeshift office and asked Lonnie, who was digging a ditch alongside some other men, to run an errand for him. Lonnie said "okay" and Cranford went ballistic.

"Boy, you don't say 'okay' to me, you say 'yes sir'—you hear me, goddamnit!" Lonnie just stood there in the ditch where he had been working, holding on tightly to his shovel like it could protect him.

"You say 'yes sir' to me damnit, SAY IT, if you want to live!" Cranford yelled at Lonnie like a rabid dog and pointed his finger in his face while Lonnie refused to open his mouth.

Kalem, who was working close by, jumped into the ditch with Lonnie after hearing Cranford carry on like a fool.

"He'll say yes sir, Mr. Cranford. He'll say it, Mr. Cranford, yes sir, he will." Kalem said repeatedly, but Lonnie still said nothing.

"He better learn if he want to stay alive. You was raised right—that boy wasn't raised right. He got to learn to say 'yes sir,'" Cranford demanded as he started back to his office.

"Yes sir, yes sir," Kalem said, "that's right." Kalem then turned to Lonnie. "Boy, you can't stay here! He'll be back just to hear you say 'yes sir.' If you can't say it, you have to leave—he is a mean son-of-a-bitch. You know I know these people! If you can't say 'yes sir' to him, you have to leave." Lonnie was smoldering in silence. Kalem continued, "YOU HEAR ME. It don't bother me to say 'yes sir,' but you have to leave," Kalem repeated. "Lonnie, you listening to me? Muh keys already in the truck, take it and leave," Kalem continued. "I'll get a way home with somebody."

"Okay." Lonnie finally opened his mouth and climbed out of the ditch to leave.

Kalem stepped out of the ditch with him and said something

to Lonnie that haunts him to this day when he thinks of what might have happened.

"Lonnie, you leave now and go straight to the truck. Don't stop walking and don't look back; if he sees you he will try to stop you, but don't stop; if he follows you, muh rifle behind the seat, you might have to KILL HIM." Kalem didn't blink an eye.

Lonnie made his way to the truck, glanced back at the rifle, and drove off. His respect for his brother deepened, as did his understanding of Uncle Jake's hatred for White people. He thought of his father's saying "yes sir" and "no sir" and recalled the time when Matt slapped him for trying to contradict a White man. He remembered the White insurance man coming to the house who was always "Mr. Bland" while his mother was "Rena." But he didn't blame his parents or his brother. He didn't even blame the bigoted Cranford. Strangely enough, he blamed the Lambs, the McNeils, the Bransfords and all the so-called good White folks who were the architects of such a hateful system.

Chapter 9
KALEM'S REDLEGS

No one ever asked if such a rule
existed… They didn't care… If it
did exist it was a bullshit rule.

The Redlegs

*T*here was limited entertainment for young adults in the country. There were the jukes on weekends, sometimes a house party somewhere, drag racing on country roads, and checker games when there was nothing else to do. The one thing that stood above all these things in the country was baseball. It was the most essential activity for every weekend and holiday, and a game could be found in each community when that team wasn't playing away from home. On Saturday mornings, country people went to town to shop, but returned in time for the games, and on Sundays they left church headed for the ball park. Anyone taking a drive through the countryside can attest to the role of baseball in the Black community.

The new high school for Blacks built in 1956, named for the White superintendent Reese McNeil, combined all the secondary schools in the county. It included a beautiful baseball field, an outside basketball court (the gymnasium came later), a football field and a cafeteria/auditorium as well as new classrooms. The new cafeteria provided hot lunches, including some for free and at reduced cost for those who qualified. At the time, it was the baseball field that drew the most interest, but in a few years football and basketball gained popularity. The new school brought all the best baseball players from all the different Black communities together in one powerful team. They won almost every game and particularly enjoyed beating the Black schools in Tisdell and the White schools in Nelms County. When the School Board desegregated the schools McNeil High School was converted to a junior high school to accommodate racist parents who didn't want their children getting diplomas from a former Black school. "Forced integration" was a two-way street that sent the Black baseball players to the White schools. A year earlier, one sports writer for the *Tisdell Times* observed after McNeil's baseball team beat a local White school in its undefeated season that Blacks won the battle but the White schools would win the war.

All the Nelms boys played high school and sandlot baseball but they were not very good at it. They were athletic enough, but neither one combined all the skills - throwing, hitting, running, fielding - required to be great players. Kalem's younger son Hank, an infielder, was probably the best in the family and Listervelt who was selected just before the girls in pickup games was the worst. Kalem even had his own team, composed of boys in the community, called the Redlegs in honor of the Cincinnati Reds. The team played behind his garage on the baseball diamond that he built, wore the baseball uniforms (white with a red stripe down the pants legs), and used the equipment (gloves, balls, bats and so on) he bought. For every game Kalem sold chicken sandwiches and fried fish, but on special occasions like July 4th he stayed up all night barbecuing hogs, goats and chickens. The famous hot dog associated with professional baseball made only a rare appearance.

After Jackie Robinson integrated baseball by joining the Brooklyn Dodgers in April, 1947, he was an instant and unrivaled hero in Nelms County. Teams all over his home state of Georgia were renamed "Dodgers" overnight and "Dodgers" versus "Dodgers" became a common occurrence. In a few months at least a dozen babies, boys and girls alike, were named Jackie. A few people in the country could tell you that Jackie Robinson won the batting title in 1949, was MVP and hit 342 the same year, but every Black person in Nelms County could tell you how he stole home on the Yankees in the 1950 World Series—and he wasn't even the best player in the Negro League. That honor belonged to Josh Gibson, who died a few months before Jackie became a Dodger. Ironically, when Larry Doby joined the Cleveland Indians of the American League only a few months later, it went virtually unnoticed among country folks. Little did anyone know that this was the beginning of the end of the Negro League.

Players and fans were good sports about losing in those days, but all losses were not equal; losing to city slickers was worse than being beat by another country team. Sometimes things got a little out of hand when a pitcher was thought to be throwing at one of the opposing team's players, since the other team was bound to retaliate at some point. Bad teams wanted to win any way they could, but the best teams cherished the competition and wanted to win fairly. In the former category was this team called the Braves in Lecompton, Georgia, about thirty miles west on highway 111 (locally Tisdell Road). According to their umpires, the Braves hit no foul balls within a few feet of the foul lines, lost no close calls running the bases, and were never allowed to strike out without taking a swipe at the ball. One home plate umpire had the habit of claiming that opposing pitchers' curve balls broke around the plate and not over it. After a while nobody played these cheaters at Lecompton; they had to book their games away from home.

A team that fell into the latter category was the Rattlers over in Orange Cove, another one of those new names Whites gave to a Black community. The Rattlers were made up almost entirely of one family—the Wales. The patriarch of the family was old man Duncan Wales who umpired every home game. His son Donnie Wales was the manager, and his sons or grandsons made up most of the team; the catcher was Duncan Wales Jr., and the pitcher was James Wales. On first base was Duncan Wales III. The second baseman was Phil Wales; third base was played by John Wales, on short stop was Cornelius Wales and in center field was Walter Wales who was called "JW" for some reason. A Garrett and a Sullivan fielded the remaining positions. The Rattlers didn't have to cheat; old man Duncan Wales expected his boys to win in a fair contest.

It was not that players themselves didn't seek an edge. Ronnie was a catcher who tried to steal an opposing team's signs. He tried one Sunday afternoon in a game between the Redlegs and the Hawks from Tisdell. In this game, Ronnie came to the plate in the ninth inning with two men on and two outs, and the Hawks leading by one run. The pitch count ran to two and two and Ronnie decided to give himself an edge by stealing the catcher's sign for the next pitch. He held out his bat with outstretched arms, lowered his head through the loop, and glanced down at the catcher's fingers as they formed the signal for what Ronnie was certain would be a curve ball. He moved his body out in front of the plate in anticipation of the curve, which had to be attacked right at the break. The pitcher, a long-armed guy, wound up tightly, glanced at the runners on second and third, turned toward the plate, and released the ball. Ronnie dug his feet in deeper, leaned his shoulders over the plate, cocked his bat to attack the speeding curve, and was hit smack dab in the mouth with a fast ball that knocked him unconscious. After his sisters applied an ice pack and cleared the blood from his mouth, Ronnie watched as his teammate Rick Washington struck out with the bases loaded. The Hawks, instead of getting on the bus and going home like they should, stayed around to gloat while the country's most attractive females made fools of themselves. As for Ronnie, he lost his front teeth and had to have surgery. He was fitted for dentures, but that didn't stop him from dropping them on the table before he ate, brushing them in his hands, and other annoying habits.

Perhaps the most memorable game the Redlegs played was in the summer of 1961 in Andersville, South Carolina. Kalem arranged the game while traveling to Andersville on occasion to deliver what he called "supplies." The sheriff up there had a terrible reputation for his treatment of Black bootleggers because he was paid to enforce the White monopoly on the trade. Each time Kalem went there, he got into an argument with his friends about who had the best baseball team. They finally decided to let the teams decide, and having lost the coin toss to determine where the game would be played, the Redlegs had to go to Andersville. The Redlegs rented this bus from Mr. Blanton, the White man who ran a bus line into Tisdell for workers who did not have cars.

The Andersville team was called the Monarchs; they said they were named for a Negro League team up north, not some White team like the Yankees or Dodgers. The Redlegs had a great following, but these Monarchs had the largest crowd the team had ever seen at a sandlot baseball game; there must have been five or six hundred people in the Andersville high school baseball stadium.

"What the hell is a Redleg?" someone hollered from the stand as the team walked onto the field to warm up.

"Y'all ain't even got the good sense to get a real name," another Monarchs fan yelled, followed by loud laughter.

"Y'all may not know what a Redleg is, but after today you will know what an ass whopping is," Pete hollered, looking right into the face of the manager Carl Staten, who fined him twenty cents—a dime for cursing and another one for getting involved with a fan.

Those Monarchs were well dressed in their white uniforms with dark blue pinstripes, matching blue socks, and a blue hat with a big "M" on the front. They looked awfully big, too. There was one pitcher in the bullpen about seven feet tall with these long rubbery arms. When he was warming up you could see the grimace on the catcher's face from the pain caused by his fastball hitting the catcher's mitt. Nobody said anything, but the Redlegs were sure relieved when he didn't trot onto the field when the game started, even though the whole team knew he was coming at some point. The Monarchs started this thin guy they called "Whiny" who looked like he was too young to be on a real team, but after a couple of warm-up tosses all doubt regarding his belonging was removed. He wound up in this tight coil like a king snake and released a rocket-like fast ball that came from the direction of first base. The Redlegs started "Baby" Wilkes who had a voice like a little boy and a fast ball that ran into the nineties.

For the first five innings, nobody scored and the fans seemed to love the excitement of a close game. In the bottom of the sixth inning this big stocky guy who played third base (the Monarchs' version of Jack Booty) hit a home run so far that it is probably still going. Baby then got the rest of the Monarchs out to end the inning, but they now led one run to zero. In the seventh inning neither team scored, which probably explains why the guy with the rubbery arm was still in the dugout. The Redlegs came to bat in the top of the eighth inning. Alfonso, the lead-off hitter and the fastest man on the team, came to bat. He hit a slow grounder to the Monarchs' shortstop, who casually played the ball, only to look up to see what every Redleg already knew; Alfonso was crossing first base before he got the ball out of his glove. Lonnie came up with a sign to bunt, but Alfonso stole second base without a throw. Good thing, too, because Lonnie watched three curve balls and went back to his seat. He could have sworn the balls curved around the plate.

Where was that Lecompton Braves umpire when you needed him? Lonnie thought.

Corey Bennett then hit a fly ball that fell in for a base hit that easily scored Alfonso. The game was now tied one to one. Ronnie shared the fate of his twin brother, which made two outs. Third baseman Pete Gammon, who had promised the Monarchs an ass-whopping, then hit a homer over the left center field wall to give the Redlegs a three- to-one lead. His fist in the air as he crossed third base would have cost him a quarter if the manager had stopped celebrating long enough to notice. The next batter, Lee Collins, struck out to end the top of the eighth inning.

In the bottom of the eighth, the Monarchs came to bat to face the Redlegs' new pitcher, Perry Dunston. Unlike Baby, Perry had this quick wind-up and then released a pitch traveling so slowly it could hardly break an egg. After a team faced Baby's fast balls for seven innings, this slow stuff was virtually unhittable. The Monarchs' first batter grounded out just before these dark clouds came from nowhere and one of these summer showers suddenly turned into a gulley-washer. So much water came down that the Redlegs ran off the field into the bullpen without waiting for the umpires to signal to stop the game. After about thirty minutes the rain slowed, but not enough to resume play, and the field was drenched. After further delay and a discussion about how far the Redlegs had to travel (about 80 miles) the umpires decided to call the game. That decision suited the Redlegs fine, since they led the game three runs to one. With 60% of the proceeds going to them (the normal split was 60% for the winners and 40% for the losers), plus a win, they couldn't have been happier.

But then all hell broke out. *The umpires declared the Monarchs the WINNERS!*

According to the officials, since the eighth inning was not completed due to rain, by rule, the game reverted to the last completed inning, which was the seventh, when the Monarchs led one run to zero. Following a few unsportsmanlike remarks, the Redlegs and Monarchs started to throw punches, and soon a fan or two got into the act. Fortunately, no one was hurt badly and the brawl ended before the police arrived, though nobody admitted to calling them in the first place. The Andersville folk didn't seem to relish the idea of giving the White sheriff the satisfaction of arresting any Black folk, even from Georgia.

The Redlegs felt cheated even though they received more than two hundred dollars from the gate. They wanted the win, not just the money. You know, no one ever asked if there were such a rule or even bothered to look it up, not even the Redlegs manager. They didn't care. Any team that was leading the Redlegs when a game ended for any reason deserved to win. That was the way of the bull. If the rule existed, it was a bullshit rule.

Chapter 10
HATTIE'S ICE CREAM

And who shall separate the dust
Which later we shall be?
Here lies the dust of Africa,
Here lies the dust of Rome.
Georgia Douglas Johnson[8]

It was a rather hot afternoon in September when a White man named James Larsen and his son Jimmy Jr. arrived at Matt's place in his old Chevy pickup truck. Matt's daughter Hattie was keeping store after school and he was in the field.

"Give me two cups of vanilla of ice cream, girl," Larsen said to Hattie.

Of all the incidents involving White people at Matt's store, this was an innocent beginning to what became the only violent confrontation. Larsen lived about five miles down the Tisdell road in a house he rented from Mr. Helgarten, who ran a large feed and seed store in Nelms county. Since the ice cream box was to the left of and not behind the counter, most customers simply helped themselves to what they wanted. Hattie wondered why this man didn't do the same thing. Nevertheless, she went to the box, reached in and got two small paper cups of vanilla ice cream, and returned behind the counter, where she took two cellophane-wrapped wooden spoons from the top of the counter, placed one of them on top of each ice cream cup and handed them to Larsen.

"Here they are," Hattie said as she handed the cups and the spoons to Larsen and held her hand out to be paid.

Larsen took the cups and spoons and gave one of each to his son.

"Daddy, open mine," the child said to his father.

Rather than open it himself, Larsen took the cup from his son and handed it to Hattie.

"Open this for my boy, girl," he said in a demanding tone.

"No! Don't open them for nobody else!" Hattie said firmly.

Hattie figured she had done enough to get the ice cream for him, since customers generally helped themselves. Besides, Hattie recognized this White man as a bigot and trouble-maker she saw when she rode to school in Tisdell. The Nelms County School Board started adding a higher grade to some of the old schools each year in the 1940s, but Matt sent his girls to a private high school, Dorsey's Academy, in Tisdell, founded by a beloved teacher named Miss Eloise Dorsey. They rode the same bus that workers took to work in the city's textile mills, a bus owned by the Blanton family. It made six trips a day, three in the morning (6, 8, and 10 a.m.) and three return trips in the evening (3, 5, and 7 p.m.). Larsen was the man Hattie and her sister Teresa saw when they caught Blanton's bus to go to Dorsey's Academy.

Black riders on Blanton's bus were required to sit behind the White riders, starting back to front while White riders were generally seated from front to back. James Larsen, whose truck was evidently unsuited for everyday use, had the habit of getting on the bus when there were few Whites and deliberately going most of the way to the back to sit down. This forced Black riders to sit behind him or stand up even though the front section of the bus was not full, thus virtually reserving most of the bus for White people. Teresa, who was a couple years older than Hattie, on a couple occasions sat in front of Larsen in defiance of the rules. When he complained, the bus driver, to his credit, made Larsen move closer to the front. Perhaps the driver realized Mr. Blanton was not paying him to risk losing his passengers. Matt scolded

Teresa when he learned about the incidents, but Teresa thought the defiance was worth the tongue-lashing.

"You damn Black wench, open this ice cream," Larsen said again, this time louder and more ominously.

"Don't open 'em for nobody else. Not going to do it for you," Hattie held her ground.

Larsen became belligerent as he reached across the counter to grab Hattie while calling her a Black "nigra" bitch, among other things. Any other of Matt's children would have opened the ice cream out of fear or to keep down trouble, but not Hattie. When Larsen reached across the counter, Hattie instinctively took the Coke bottle that she was drinking from, turned it around to grip the neck, wasting the remainder of its contents on her dress, and with all her power planted the bottom part of the Coca-Cola bottle right above Larsen's left ear, squarely on his temple. Blood gushed out from Larsen's head like a wide-open faucet and he hit the floor like a sack of potatoes.

Hattie was almost seventeen years old and already had some history of reacting with violence. Boys who came to the store to see the girls claimed that Hattie was mean and learned not to mess around with her. Grady Wilson summed up Hattie's attitude after she slapped him for putting his hands where she thought they had no business: "Hattie took no shit, at no time, from nobody," he declared.

One day some boys were playing with "fire poppers" (firecrackers) they had bought and Catherine recalled what happened. "Someone lit one and threw it under Hattie's legs, and she took a bucket and hit him across the head with it. Daddy came down to the store to get after the boy about it, but when he got there, the boy was bleeding so, and Daddy started feeling sorry for him and did not say a word."

From Hattie's perspective, the issue with Larsen was not racial but personal. He was demanding that she do something she did not want to do, and then he had the audacity to try to put his hands on her.

Hattie's brother Andrew was in the store at the time of the incident, along with their cousin Horace Wilburn, a stocky man who talked much among Black folk, but completely lost his tongue in the presence of Whites. Horace was the one person who could drink a Coke and eat a bag of peanuts (pouring the peanuts into the bottle) in such a way that you wanted to do the same thing, but when you did the taste failed to live up to the expectation. Cousin Horace just stood there in paralyzed disbelief at what he had witnessed, while Andrew rushed out of the store as fast as he could toward the field where Matt was working to get him to come to the store.

It took a while for the implications of what had happened to sink in, but when they did, Hattie was frightened. James Larsen began to stir after a few minutes as his son cried uncontrollably. Hattie managed to gain her composure, took a cloth that was normally used for dusting, and filled it with ice from the box to make an ice pack. She placed it against Larsen's head and told him to hold it against the wound, because she certainly wasn't going to do it for him.

In a couple of minutes Larsen was up and moving slowly out of the store toward his truck, holding a bloody rag up to his head and calling Hattie all kinds of bitches and promising to be back to teach her a lesson all "nigger bitches" ought to know about how to treat good White people. Larsen's self-assessment did not square with other opinions; he was one of those White people that other Whites considered "poor white trash," though most Blacks found it difficult to understand why people called other human beings "trash." Larsen was certainly no gentleman of property and standing in this county. He liked to hang around Black people, but had no friends among them and didn't seem to have many White friends either. He seemed to wallow in the deference so many

Black people paid to his kind.

Matt came hurriedly to the store from the field some distance away, as Andrew galloped behind him. By the time he arrived, Larsen and his son had left. Hattie, Andrew, and Horace, who had regained his tongue, all tried simultaneously to tell Matt what happened.

"All y'all shut up," Matt said after hearing enough to discern the essentials of what had happened. He turned to Hattie and asked, "Why, Hattie? Why is opening a cup of ice cream going to kill you? Why?"

"Don't open it for nobody else!" Hattie said again.

"Do you know what could happen now, Hattie? Do you know that cracker [the meanest word Matt ever uttered about White people] could even get the Klan in here. They could burn down the store and our house and worse. All we can do now is be prepared. I will deal with you later, Hattie," Matt said.

Matt went up the hill to the house as Rena who had come down to the store walked along beside him.

"Don't open ice cream for nobody else," Hattie mumbled.

It was not long before many neighbors had left the fields or returned from work and learned what had happened. One by one they came to ask if they could help—one or two with shotguns they used for hunting. Only a few owned pistols. Soon most of the neighbors were gathered—the Garretts, Dentons, Williams, and Matt's brothers. The children were sent up the hill to the house until this thing blew over—or blew up.

The neighbors knew that they could defend themselves, but what if the law came which was always on the side of White people—that included no-good Jimmy Larsen. Deep down inside, they knew Matt was not going to let anybody, not even the law, take Hattie away without him. But what if the law did not come, and some White man was killed in self-defense? The shooter could still be imprisoned or even lynched. The suggestion that they send for the sheriff to try to "nip the thing in the bud" was rejected immediately, but the idea of sending for Mr. Kin, or even Mr. Bransford took a lot longer to dismiss. But this was Matt's daughter they were talking about; if they could not help his family, who could they stand up for?

They waited. Seven p.m. came, then 8, then 9, 10 and 11 came and went. Some thought: "The Klan coming at midnight."

"Them cowards just waiting for midnight. Dey wants dere Negroes in bed. Dat's the way of cowards, but tonight dey gits a surprise," Walter Garrett muttered.

Morning came and they were still sitting there, several of them asleep with their guns behind their chairs, but no one came and nothing happened. With the advent of dawn, a great sigh of relief descended over the neighborhood. Matt thanked everybody as they left for home. Rena got up, made breakfast, and prepared the kids for school. The girls, including Hattie, didn't have to ride the Blanton bus today. Matt took them into Tisdell in his truck just in case Larsen was on the bus to try to start trouble.

Black people this day were thankful to God, for they saw His hand in what happened, or did not happen, and Matt prayed a thankful prayer for such great friends. Those who were reluctant to see God's intervening hand thought perhaps Whites didn't think poor White trash was worth defending. Some assumed White people felt that this was one sorry White man, can't defend himself from one young Colored gal. Others thought perhaps it was Matt, his reputation as a good man, but most would not have waged money on this position. Perhaps they remembered the words of Rev. Whatley:

"Whites can't always tell the difference between good and bad Negroes. There are Negroes who don't drink, but when one is drunk, the whole race is drunk. "

Many thought this might be one of those times, but they didn't come and these were some relieved Black people on this day in Nelms County.

About two weeks later in the late afternoon, just before dark, there was a group of adults standing outside Matt's store talking and some kids playing. They included Matt, Hattie, Uncle Walton, Teresa, "Uncle" Tommy, and some of the neighbors and their children. At a distance, they could see a long line of cars coming up Tisdell city road with the lights on like a funeral procession, but they had an eerie feeling that told them this was no funeral.

When the cars got close enough for them to see the lead car, it had a great big gold cross in front. The cross, attached to the grille and hood between the headlights, stood above the roofline of the car and was all lit up even though it was not quite dark. On the roof and the trunk of the car were large Confederate battle flags waving tall in the wind. The lead car was followed by about ten other cars with smaller Confederate battle flags, all filled with what can only be assumed to be White men, since they were wearing white hoods over their heads. Most of the people in front of Matt's store were frightened and went inside the store and stared out the door and window. For a second it looked like the KKK had decided to come after all, but the cars kept on going past the store. No one ever figured out exactly where they were going, though many thought they were going to Little Mountain in Lecompton or even Stone Mountain near Atlanta where Klan rallies were held. The Cranford family was surely among them. Most likely they were going to one of their farms for a big meeting and cross-burning. It didn't matter where they were headed; all were happy just to see them keep going.

Hattie watched until the last car was well out of sight and mumbled, "don't open em for nobody else."

Chapter 11

MISS PLEUTSY'S YANG-YANG

*I*t was near midnight on the day Hattie struck Jimmy Larsen when Miss Pleutsy, the midwife and conjure woman, arrived at the Nelms household to offer her assistance. The neighbors, most of whom objected to her presence, had gathered much earlier to offer their help to the family. Living farther back in the woods than the other neighbors, she had just heard from Mary Garrett, a woman seeking her help in a delicate matter, that Hattie had hit a White man on the head with a Coke bottle. Miss Pleutsy brought an ankle bracelet to assure Hattie would not be taken away and a potion to protect her from the White demons. Matt decided against Miss Pleutsy's kind of help and politely explained that she could remain, but her conjure things must be removed from the premises. Miss Pleutsy left the house and walked down across the road to the grocery store, convincing herself on the way that her remedy would be more effective at the place where the incident took place. She found a Pepsi-Cola crate to sit down on and dozed off-and-on for the rest of the night. When morning came Miss Pleutsy noticed relieved neighbors leaving and she felt assured of the efficacy of her methods. A few weeks later she heard that the KKK had passed Matt's store going to a big meeting and was excited to learn that her concoction underneath the store window was still a potent force.

It was a tradition in Black communities for someone to serve as midwife, healer, and even conjuror. This tradition extended back to slavery days, though the knowledge of herbal medicines went back farther to the West African homeland. Even the well-known underground railroader Harriet Tubman was an herbalist who administered paregoric to young children to keep them quiet while fleeing from slavery; adults she threatened to shoot when freedom wasn't drug enough for them. Miss Pleutsy's mother, Hilda Grayson, served the Nelms County Black community for almost four decades as granny midwife and "doctor." She was affectionately known as "Miss Hilda," a name she had earned years before she married the peg-legged David Grayson. Miss Hilda was a lady about the size of Gama Staten and shared her color, hair and temperament. She often wore a long dirndl skirt tight around the waist like a broomstick full at the hemline. Her skilled hands had attended too many births to count. Her wise counsel comforted frightened mothers, her folk medicine warded off pain, and her gentle spirit reassured worried fathers that a healthy son or daughter would soon grace their household. Occasionally her expertise even extended beyond medicine to affairs of the heart. When she died in the fall of 1945, her funeral was one of the largest anyone could remember in Nelms County.

Her loss saddened the community, but most of her services had been taken over by her daughter, Neficent, who came to be known as "Miss Pleutsy." Miss Pleutsy was a midwife, but she preferred the world of conjuring and mysticism, which militated against her acquiring the exalted status of her mother. Besides, the state of Georgia had required her to take courses of study under the White doctor, John Bransford, during the early 1940s to be certified as a midwife. She objected to those with book learning looking over her shoulders, judging what she had learned from her mother and grandmother.

"All the knowledge of all the doctors in the world can't equal the medicine God done put in His roots," she said.

State-sanctioned encroachment on her midwifery had lead Miss Pleutsy increasingly into the world of voodoo and root work. In addition, more and more Black women were going to the segregated hospital at Tisdell to give birth or sending for one of the city's three Black doctors. By the middle of the century, midwives were losing their sacred place in the African-American community. Even the last one of Matt's and Rena's thirteen children had been delivered at the Tisdell Hospital in 1948. Increasingly, those who were down on their luck, or needed to deal with a nasty neighbor or to control a lying, cheating wife or husband, found in Miss Pleutsy a most helpful resource. She had a yang-yang thing to remedy most any bad situation.

When attending a pregnant mother, Miss Pleutsy carried a small hatchet which she claimed cut the pain when placed under the bed of the woman in labor.

"When the apple gets ripe it's gonna fall, and nothing to stop it except me to catch it," she said.

After the baby was born, Miss Pleutsy took the afterbirth (placenta) and burned it in the fireplace or a fire outside to prevent it from being hexed by some evil doer.

She delivered over 500 babies, including Lonnie and Ronnie. She thought that twins were good luck, especially since they both came feet first, and dismissed the superstitious few who thought multiple births brought bad luck. She felt anytime you had a healthy child, it was good; two made it twice as good. Rumor had it also that Miss Pleutsy performed a service for young girls who got into trouble because people claimed to have seen some White people leaving her house late at night. Whites had no monopoly on this procedure, but religious beliefs and expense sometimes put the practice out of reach for many Black girls who bore their children and the consequences. Perhaps the state's "meddling" in child delivery not only forced Miss Pleutsy into root work, but also into what some Black people at the time considered a sordid business.

Generally, respectable Black folk had no time for Miss Pleuty's conjuring, and they kept a healthy distance from it. For these people, God offered the only spiritual intervention they needed, and they were perfectly capable of calling on Him all by themselves, thank you. Nelms County already had a full-time root worker who was named professionally for a scavenger. Dr. Crow was a native resident of the county, having been born Ernest Dotson in Drayton. At a young age, his family moved to Macon County, where he grew up and began a career as a preacher before his congregation got word of his root doctoring and forced him out of the church. Since he was not inclined to leave of his own volition, church members engaged the services of the local White sheriff. Dotson returned to a remote part of Nelms County where he plied his trade full time on the more superstitious among poor Black and White people.

Matt did not always welcome Miss Pleutsy to his home as he had Miss Hilda, so she visited Rena when Matt was in the store or out doing business—which in honesty was most of the time. Children often had the run of the neighborhood, which in the country could be a mile or more in any direction, but Miss Pleutsy's house, located about a quarter of a mile back in the woods where the children called the sticks, was off limits. During her visits, she advised Rena to keep her clothesline sprinkled with one of her potions so nobody could hex her clothes, and she gave her a potion to put around the doors and windows to keep the evil spirits out of the house. Of course, she had to go through the house first with her yang-yang thing to run all evil out.

"The worst thing that can happen is to trap an evil spirit in the house—sickness, mental disease, miscarriages, desertion, all caused by such a thing," Miss Pleutsy advised.

Rena didn't put much stock in roots, but she liked Pleutsy—she never used the "Miss"—and indulged her when she came to visit.

Still pending was the matter of Mary Garrett, whose problem had been put on hold after she informed Miss Pleusty of Hattie's troubles. Mary had now returned for Miss Pleutsy's assistance. She explained her suspicions that her husband of ten years had been cheating on her with another woman, though she lacked the usual evidence – lipstick on his collar, lack of sexual interest, staying out all night, and so on — but for almost a month now she had been unable to stop her left breast from itching, a sure sign somebody was trying to get her man. Miss Pleusty wondered what fake conjurors had led her to such a superstition. She reassured Mary that she was in complete control and would handle the situation as soon as possible. Mary stood up to leave, expressed her gratitude by pressing a ten in Miss Pleutsy's palm, and departed, walking down the puddle-filled walkway to the gate that led away from Miss Pleutsy's house. She slowly disappeared around the bend of the road to go to her house.

The next morning, Miss Pleutsy stepped outside to sniff the morning air and concluded that this summer was going to be gentle, not too hot, about right. She slammed shut her screen door and latched the hook. Her small dark-brown frame made its way through her house lighting incense, as she did every morning and became fussier every day as she grew older about letting in God's light. Her cat Caution followed close behind, behaving more like a dog than a cat.

Miss Pleutsy got dressed and went out. She wore a long white dress that kind of flowed in the wind and brought out her dark complexion. Although it was early, children were already playing hopscotch and marbles and riding bikes while others ran behind waiting for a chance to ride them. Over the hill she saw boys sliding down the steep hills on car tires. Farther away in the distance a pickup baseball game was being organized. As she met a couple neighbors on the way to work they bowed and nodded at a distance as she walked across the ground to the Tisdell road. She always walked like she was on a definite mission, and with her head way up in the air like she was Head Angel, or at least one of God's special creatures.

"Miss Pleutsy," someone called out to her. "Uum, Miss

Pleutsy."

Miss Pleutsy turned around to see that it was Bussey Newton's bright smiling face, yellow teeth and unkempt body. Today, he was wearing the tie around his neck that generally hung from the pocket of his coat. Virtually everybody called him "crazy" because he roamed the neighborhood talking to himself and waving his arms, but Miss Pleutsy never treated him that way. If she said it once she said it a thousand times: "All God's creatures deserve respect."

"Miss Pleutsy ... no soun fer me... you gon have the package for me?" Combat asked while he continued to mumble to himself.

"Yeah, Mr. Newton, I'll have it for you today." Miss Pleutsy knew the children and some adults had started calling him "Combat," but she never did.

Combat thanked her and walked off in the direction of the place where he lived, still in acrobatic mode. Miss Pleutsy never knew what package that he referred to, but she always said "yes," knowing that he would come back the next day only to ask the same question. No matter how many times he asked, he never came back looking to pick up anything, just to ask the question. At last, Miss Pleutsy arrived at Matt's store where she picked up some liniments and the like that she had Matt get from Mr. Stocks. What she didn't buy, she grew in her herb garden or found in the woods. Children claimed they saw her digging in the woods and praying in the church's cemetery. She was no doubt harvesting medicinal roots and thanking the ancestors for their wisdom.

Miss Pleutsy returned home with the items she picked up from Matt's store. The day had passed quickly, and she retired for the night to reflect on the changing times, not just the summer giving way to fall or new life coming to replace old, but the culture was changing. The young had little respect for Miss Pleutsy's work though they still feared her some. She thought, *This generation don't respect old age as they should.* The children—even those whom she had helped to deliver—were turning on her with pranks and taunts. How long before she would move on, she didn't know, but if the elders had kept their teachings, she would have lived forever on the tongues of many generations.

In the afternoon of the next day, Miss Pleutsy had walked almost an hour on the Tisdell road before she was picked up by a truck driver who gave her a ride to town. When she walked into The Buick Club, she looked out of place among the crowd of people. Over the din of the bar she heard the person she was searching for before she could see his face in the dark barroom. She made her way to Robert Garrett, who was hanging on to a skinny, skimpily dressed, high yella gal with too little hair for a woman, and smiling with more teeth than were meant for one mouth.

"Mr. Garrett," Miss Pleutsy called from the dark of the smoke-filled room.

"Who is that calling me?" Garrett squinched his eyes trying to see who the shadowy figure was calling him.

"If you don't do right by that woman of yours, you bound to die from her unhappiness," Miss Pleutsy said from the shadows.

Garrett put the glass of whiskey down on the table, wasting its contents on the tablecloth and yelling to Miss Pleutsy, "get that damn voodoo stuff out of here, old woman."

Miss Pleutsy went out the back door rather than try to find her way to the front entrance where she came in. The door slammed shut as a Lightning Hopkins blues record started on the juke box, which coughed out the message: "Do right by your woman or she will do wrong by you."

About a week later Miss Pleutsy was sweeping her floor when she looked up and saw Mary Garrett standing at her gate dressed in black for mourning, a veil hung just below her forehead. She went out to greet her, but wisely decided to remain silent. They both walked away toward the herb garden, exactly matching each other's steps like members of a secret society on a funeral march. Evidently Mary had failed to contemplate all the possibilities of her request for help. Miss Pleutsy never claimed to be a mind reader, but she had been plying her trade long enough to recognize buyer's remorse when she saw it.

Miss Pleutsy left her mark despite modern times encroaching on the ways of the country. She died several years later, gliding into the arms of the spirits of her mother, grandmother, and other ancestors. Unlike Miss Hilda's funeral, which brought out most of the Black and some White people in the county, Miss Pleutsy's rites were scarcely attended and some members of Mt. Canaan were even hesitant about holding the service there and burying her in the church's cemetery. In the conversations of Nelms County, the mention of Miss Pleutsy's name elicited respect, but also apprehension, which bubbled over when Gail Grayson, showing a remarkable resemblance to Miss Pleutsy, showed up claiming to be Miss Pleutsy's daughter. Nobody ever heard that she had any children, and the people were quite certain she never had a husband. Some say it was a younger Miss Pleutsy who had come back from the dead – reincarnated – no one said she was "resurrected," as that was too sacred. Be that as it may, Gail produced sufficient papers to convince the authorities that she was Miss Pleutsy's offspring and they gave her rights to all her possessions, including her little house. Gail moved into the home and let it be known that she was open for business by hanging out a huge, brightly lit sign with a large palm on it. It seemed only one or two local persons sought her help or friendship, and except for a few customers from out of town she lived there mostly in isolation. Miss Pleusty's cat Caution returned, but refused to live in the house. It seems he too never warmed up to "Madam Gail."

Chapter 12
SAY AMEN ... LIGHTS

The Negro church, although not a
shadow of what it ought to be,
is the great asset of the race.

Carter G. Woodson[9]

There were more than a dozen Black Baptist churches serving Nelms County, but there were no Black Methodists, Episcopalians, Catholics, Presbyterians or Muslims, Black or otherwise. About half of the churches were named "mount" something such as Mt. Olivet, Mt. Calvary, Mt. Canaan, and Mt. Holyoke; the largest church turned the name around to become Rose Mount. There was no elite church in the country, but a member of Rose Mount might have claimed otherwise in a case of perception trumping reality. Church services were held only once a month; on other Sundays, members attended neighboring churches, and pastors generally had four churches. When well-liked ministers preached anniversaries and revivals at different churches, people followed them like celebrities. Their members bragged about who was the best preacher, who had the best voice, who wore the best suit, and who drove the newest car; women even discussed who was the best-looking, which in some cases meant the lightest-skinned.

Mt. Canaan Missionary Baptist Church, the Nelms family church, met on third Sundays and almost everybody in the community was a member. Virtually every rural Black man and woman was a God-fearing Christian. The most notable exceptions in the Nelms family were Matt's brother Jake and his son Kalem, a fact that deeply saddened Matt. Kalem, somewhat of an agnostic, was not in the same category as Jake, who was more than a mere atheist; he joked that God sat up in a big tree and watched over everybody. He was a blasphemer whom God was bound to punish. When he went to jail for murder, everybody knew the chickens had come home to roost.

All Black churches held soul-saving revivals each summer and fall that attracted throngs of people to charismatic preaching, soul-stirring singing, and great praying. There were no air conditioners in those days, and the paper fans provided by Tisdell's Black funeral homes offered little relief. Those trying to get saved, ordinarily eleven and twelve-year old children, sat on the Mourner's Bench (a pew in the front of the sanctuary designated for them) where they could be singled out for prayer by deacons; if they had a special interest in one mourner, they prayed particularly hard for him or her to join the church. Old people claimed that one's sins belonged to your parents until age twelve, and parents were obligated to get their children converted while they could still absorb their sins.

When Matt was a boy, he failed to get off the Mourners' Bench for years and his grandmother Murrh prayed daily for him to be saved. Matt sat on that bench twelve or thirteen times, every fall and summer beginning at age eleven, and the neighbors were worried he would never accept Christ, being so old, that is, and prayed for him. Finally, at age seventeen Matt was saved, but not by the traditional route. One day, Matt's grandmother said she had a vision of a child who appeared before her in white soap suds, and the vision, she believed, was an angel who said that a child had been cleansed. A few minutes later, Matt came in to say that he had been saved by the Holy Ghost. At the next Sunday service, Matt confessed, and a special baptism was held for him at Eucheche Creek the following week.

All the Nelms children were saved and joined Mt. Canaan

while their sins belonged to their parents. Lonnie and Ronnie sat on the Mourners' Bench the first time when they twelve years old, with three other boys and two girls. One of the boys, Rufus Jenkins, a thin, dark-complexioned fellow who lived about as far in the woods as Miss Pleutsy, always seemed to be smiling. On the second night of the revival, Rufus, in the middle of the preacher's sermon, stood straight up and fell just as straight to the floor and lay there jerking his arms back and forth, kicking his feet, and flailing around to an onslaught of "praise the Lords." By the time the ushers and deacons surrounded Rufus, Lonnie was unable to see what was happening and he stood up on the Mourners' Bench to get a better view. At that point someone yelled out, "ANOTHER ONE," to a chorus of Amen. When Lonnie realized they were talking about him, he quickly sat back down. The ushers finally restrained Rufus before he calmed down and sat in one of the chairs provided for those who were saved. He then told the congregation that he was now a believer and wished to be baptized by water as he had been by the Holy Spirit.

The next night one of the girls repeated this act, except a female usher seemed to have been previously assigned the specific duty of keeping her dress from flying above her waist. That same night Ronnie got off the Mourners' Bench, but without any of the gymnastics. Lonnie did not get off until the last night of the revival, Friday. He thought then he had to get off or he had to do it again next year and Ronnie would be ahead of him, so he got off. By this time, the church had put in a baptismal pool in front of the sanctuary behind the pulpit, and this group of converts was first to be baptized in it. The old people would tell you that the church lost some of its spirit, even the ole time religion, when the congregation stopped dressing in white and singing while they marched down to Eucheche Creek for baptism.

Easter was the holiest day of the year, but the kids didn't get gifts, only new clothes, like they did at Christmas, so they preferred

His birth to His resurrection. The pastor always preached a long sermon about crucifixion and salvation, but if the truth be told, a twelve-year-old didn't understand much about such things as communion where people drank Jesus' blood and ate His body. They liked the Easter egg hunt but didn't understand its significance, any more than they did communion. The area of the hunt included the cemetery, even though superstitions kids were afraid the ghosts of dead people might jump out at them or grab their legs—one of those bridge men—and not let go. They also had to be careful because they understood it was bad luck to step on a grave, and they knew that pointing at a grave made your finger rot off. Then there was also the fear of snakes in the grass which had not been cut closely to make it easier to hide the eggs.

The church provided more than spiritual benefits to families in need. The most important help was through benevolent societies which members called the "ciety." Members paid dues of 25-50 cents and received sick benefits when they were ill and burial expenses when they passed. Mt. Canaan had three of these organizations, and most people belonged to all three even though a single membership carried the entire family. When people got sick the members had to visit them, and if they had no family, a member, taking turns alphabetically, stayed with them until they were well. Matt didn't trust some members, because there was the time Shirley Morgan was supposed to be sick and had received $20 from the society, but when he visited her, she was plowing the field like a man.

The Old People's Benevolent Society met at Matt's store each year on its anniversary to give out goods to its members. For the occasion Matt stocked his store with flour, soap, lard, meal, sugar, molasses, and other foods. He and Deacons Sam Denton, Richard Thomas, and Sturgis Smith got together before the anniversary and put one of each item in a big box and loaded them on a truck. Each box was referred to as "one time." On the day of the anniversary all the society members gathered at Matt's store. The president of the "ciety" climbed on the truck with a roster of members and called out the names of family heads and the "times."

"Robert Dunn, six times."

"Samuel Denton, ten times."

"Jack Levitt, four times."

"Matt Nelms, fourteen times."

What this meant was that every family would get "one time" for each member of the family. Matt's family was fourteen "times," twelve children, and "one time" for Matt and "one time" for Rena—"fourteen times." Old people said that this was the era when people looked out for each other in the community before there was welfare.

In the country there was egalitarianism that transcended class and color. This was not difficult to understand in the absence of hierarchical organizations (e.g., fraternities and sororities) that structured relationships and occupations (doctors and lawyers) that produced significant wealth. Teaching was probably the most respected occupation, but businessmen probably exercised the most influence outside the community. Ministers with good reputations were probably second to teachers, but a few did not have good reputations. Buddy Williams disliked ministers because when he was growing up the minister came to his house when his daddy wasn't home and his mother made him go outside to play. Ralph Jones recalled the minister would show up at supper time and his parents would feed him first. The preacher "sat himself down at the table," according to Ralph, and "ate up all the food." When he left, his mother had to try to find food for the rest of the family. Ralph and Buddy became trustees at Mt. Canaan to sabotage the pastor's agenda.

When Lonnie began teaching at the local high school, members of Mt. Canaan tried for several years to get him to research and read the church history for its anniversary program. In truth, church members were pleased with what they had, but they wanted him to read it to give it the appearance of authenticity, having a school teacher do it. As for Lonnie's part, he thought the request was a ploy to get him to come to church on a regular basis. He had heard the history read many times:

> Mt. Canaan began in 1886 when eight Christian soldiers withdrew from the Holyoke Baptist Church. They were led by Deacons Howard Denton and Lee Williams until the first pastor was named in 1888. The same year he added 30 new souls to the church. Great soul-stirring revivals were led by Reverend Walter Williams until his resignation in 1926 after more than thirty years of service. Over a period of fifteen years, four ministers served the church until Rev. Horace Whatley was named pastor in 1942. Sister Lou Ann Green gave a picture to the church and Deacon Jones bought the first communion glasses. In 1942 Deacon Jones bought a pew for the church. Rev. Whatley raised $60 in 1945 for a church picnic. Sister Louise Goddard in 1945 helped form the beautification club and the Williams Choir was organized. The Denton family gave two pews to the church. Rev. Jones started the gospel choir, James Merritt started the Trustee Board etc., etc. This is the story of one church built upon a rock so the gates of hell may not prevail against it.

Lonnie had no intention of reading half an hour of this kind of stuff. He also knew that if he changed it to look like a "real history," he might as well move to another county. These old folks had heard their family names mentioned for the past thirty years and would not take their omission lightly.

Rena promised Reverend Horace Whatley that Lonnie would work on the history and set out to prevail upon him to do it. Reverend Whatley had little education, like most rural Black ministers, but he dressed like a professor. He wore a fedora like Matt, a pinstriped suit and a vest with a watch and chain that gave him the look of W. E. B. DuBois or some other college professor.

"Lonnie, I promised the pastor that you would come see him," Rena informed Lonnie. "He wants you to do the church history."

"Mama, you know I don't want to get involved in that kind of thing," Lonnie said emphatically.

"I done told him you would," she said. "I done give him my word."

With Mama Rena now involved, having given her "word," Lonnie soon caved in and said that he would look at it. After a conversation with Pastor Whatley, he agreed to do the history, but he was puzzled that the pastor asked him to attend the deacons' meeting on Friday night, where it would be put to a vote. It was approved only after a few more confusing comments about the danger of digging into the past.

Lonnie read over the history given to him and decided he would simply clean it up—correct the grammar, give a little historical context, and highlight the most salient facts, that sort of thing. Doing this was not easy, since he was left with a history that was much too long to read in a hot church on a Sunday afternoon in July during a three-hour service. After some soul searching, Lonnie devised what he considered a brilliant plan. He decided to do *TWO* histories, a short one that he would read aloud in church, and a longer one with all the names and trivia that would be printed in the anniversary program for all to take home as a memento. That way everyone would be happy.

The church history showed that Mt. Canaan grew out of a

schism—a euphemism for a knock-down, drag-out fight with a neighboring church, the Holyoke Baptist Church. This came as no surprise to Lonnie, who had witnessed some of the arguments in Mt. Canaan's church conferences where every position had scripture on its side. He remembered one conference he attended when the deacons of the church decided to add an educational building, but to save money they agreed to put in air conditioning later. Lonnie suggested that the duct work ought to be completed at the time of the construction so that it would be less expensive when the central air conditioner was added. Most deacons and trustees thought his suggestion was reasonable, but Deacon Walker Diggs reminded them that they had set a deadline that could not be changed. As he put it: "We done already set a deadline —you can't change a deadline. Why do you think they call it a *d-e-a-d* line?"

On another occasion, Lonnie attended a conference where he learned that all the church's funds were kept in a non-interest-bearing checking account. This time he asked the church to consider putting its money in an account that paid interest, or setting up two accounts, one for operating expenses like the present account, and another for its savings that paid interest. Deacon Willie Bussey pointed out that interest was *evil*, and Lonnie with his education wanted Black churches to be like White churches. Lonnie then recommended that the church give the "evil interest" to charity; that way Mt. Canaan would not be tainted by "evil interest." When this proposition failed, he vowed to leave them to themselves. Now here he was involved in this history.

Due to these positions, Lonnie *was* surprised by the church's ability to maintain pastors. In over eighty years, the church had only six or seven pastors, two of whom, including Rev Whatley, had a combined service of about sixty years. When he charted the pastors with the dates of service, curiously one minister was missing for the years around 1938 to1942. Lonnie was puzzled because the omission was not due to an absence of records because of a fire, flood, or some other disaster. The gap puzzled Lonnie, but he was determined not to get further involved.

The anniversary came on July 21st and was held at 2:00 p.m., after the morning service. The devotion lasted about an hour with the raising of several hymns and three prayers. They were followed by the welcome, announcements, songs by the choir, an altar call, and two collections, one for the poor and another for tithes. These things took place with a master of ceremony (MC) adlibbing in between. It was now time to read the history. After being introduced by the MC, the crowded church came to a hush as Lonnie began.

"The History of the Mount Canaan Missionary Baptist Church." He began with a familiar scripture to set the congregation at ease: "Upon this rock, I will build my church and the gates of hell shall not prevail against it." He read slowly and carefully.

In about ten minutes, Lonnie had finished reading. He had talked briefly about the role of religion, had explained the church as a multi-faceted institution, and had sprinkled in a few important names. It was not his fault that one of the names was his father, Matt Nelms, who had donated land and negotiated the loan for a new sanctuary. Nevertheless, by the time Lonnie finished, the congregation had lapsed into a White funeral mode. He thought that they had not heard him say, "thank you" at the end of his reading so he repeated it more emphatically: "Thank you."

It seemed much longer to Lonnie, but for about fifteen seconds there was dead silence; an absolute first, not a single amen. Lenny thought, *Say amen … lights.*

As he moved back to his seat there was sporadic applause, out of respect for the teacher, not the history. Lonnie's worst fears were realized.

After Rev. Whatley's familiar sermon on sin and damnation,

the service concluded and Lonnie tried quietly to make his way outside before he could be cornered by some church member. He didn't make it.

"Boy, you think your family de only one done something in this church," Wilhemina Bussey uttered.

"If you can't do the histry right, you oughtn't do it at all," Roberta Diggs condemned.

The whole Duncan family passed the Nelms family without a word. Lonnie handed the history to Rena and asked her to give it to the pastor, thinking she got him into this mess.

"Didn't these people see the program with all those names on it, Mama?" Lonnie muttered.

"Want 'em read. Didn't you see all those visitors? Want 'em read—where is your common sense?" Rena said.

Lonnie walked away, thinking how foolish he had been to get involved in the first place.

A few weeks passed and that missing pastor started nagging at Lonnie. Since the whole thing was now over, he could now satisfy his curiosity. He went down to see his oldest sister Elizabeth, who had moved home from Philadelphia.

"Boy, you don't know that story?" Elizabeth asked Lonnie.

"No, why should I?" Lonnie said.

"You know about Queen, don't you?" she asked. "Some of this real personal," she said, but did not wait for an answer. "Your Aunt Queen by marriage, your Uncle Jake's wife. She was your blind Aunt, blind and beautiful," Elizabeth emphasized.

"Well, I vaguely remember hearing about Uncle Jake having a blind wife who used to sing in church," Lonnie said as he strained to remember.

"That's Queen. She died before you were born. She could play the piano like she was born with the thing in her hand and had the most melodious voice that I had ever seen," Elizabeth said.

"You mean 'heard.'" Lonnie forgot himself for a moment.

Elizabeth did not like to be corrected, especially when you obviously knew what she meant.

"Well, the man who was pastor of Mount Canaan during those years was Reverend Andrew David White. God knows how he became a Baptist preacher, and pastor of this church!

The man could not carry a tune in a bucket. He was as tone deaf as Queen was blind." Laughing heartily, Elizabeth continued, "boy you know how helpless a Baptist preacher is without a song to sing?" Elizabeth went on.

She seemed to want Lonnie to answer, but all he could think of was how some people said that about her; she couldn't sing a lick either, and she tried to preach.

"I guess," Lonnie said finally.

"You guess? He is like a centipede that doesn't know what leg to move. A Baptist preacher who can't sing, that's one of those 'moron' things, isn't it." Elizabeth paused.

"I don't know what an oxymoron got to do with..."

Elizabeth interrupted before Lonnie finished. She particularly did not like being told that an oxymoron was not "a moron thing." It reminded Lonnie of Uncle Walton who used to say "forest," when he really meant "farce." Elizabeth always spoke with great authority, her words sounding like the unchallenged truth. She did not want agreement, she needed only to know that you were listening, and a simple head nod would do.

"Uh huh." Lonnie managed.

"Rev. A. D. who couldn't sing a lick got Queen to sing for him. She was the voice that he never had. They went everywhere together. With his preaching and her singing and playing he became the preacher he could not be without a tune. He even preached at the great Tabernacle in Tisdell. Queen knew exactly when to start playing or singing, their timing was perfect." She digressed again. "In some churches pianos were too secular, but Mt. Canaan had one way back in the 1930s."

Lonnie said nothing, realizing that she had deviated and needed to find her way back.

"I loved Queen. She was so pretty. She followed that preacher and that no-good sinner fooled her. He got her pregnant and denied it. You can't say this, boy, but Rev. White is Listervelt's real daddy. Queen married your uncle Jake and he treated that child just like his own. Velt probably don't even know and don't need to know about this. When the church put that preacher out, he left and nobody ever heard from him again. "You listening boy?" Elizabeth asked.

"Yeah, I'm listening. That is a sad story. So the church wiped the slate clean. How could they pretend he was never there?" Lonnie asked.

"They burned the records – anything with his name on it. Yes sir, sure enough did, had to burn the records to cleanse the sin from the church. The pulpit was uh … you know, made holy again," Elizabeth said.

"Consecrated?" Lonnie couldn't help himself.

"Your missing preacher isn't missing no more. Don't you go talking to Velt. I know you're like brothers. Jake the only daddy he needs to know about. Why you think Jake don't go to church? He hates preachers. Jake refused to get married in the church, had to go to the courthouse," Elizabeth said.

Lonnie was saddened by this turn of events. Perhaps it was Listervelt living the lie that saddened him.

"Velt's mother died in childbirth, didn't she?" Lonnie asked.

"She sure did. She and Jake got married soon as it was found out about the preacher. Jake loved Queen even before that preacher ruined her." Elizabeth felt drained.

Lonnie now understood why there was so much grumbling about digging into the past. Nevertheless, at the next church conference he recommended that the minister's name be restored to Mt. Canaan's history. He argued that history cannot be wiped away because of some wrong that occurred or sanitized because times have changed. Can we pretend slavery never existed? Over some objections, Lonnie's resolution carried to restore Rev. Andrew David White's name to the list of pastors. At least Lonnie felt he had accomplished something, but nobody ever asked him to read the history again.

Chapter 13

THE GIRL IN CHANDELIER EARRINGS

Love is like a seed, it does not choose
the ground on which it falls.

African Proverb[10]

*L*istervelt was over six feet tall, skinny and somewhat frail-looking as a boy, but hardier than people realized. He was a couple years older than Lonnie and Ronnie, the same age as Lil Kal. He wasn't as popular as most boys his age, because he kept to himself and didn't share the same interest in sports. He was a smart kid who preferred reading a book to throwing a baseball and was called a "sissy" because he didn't always act like his peers. His name didn't help much either as Listervelt became "Listerine," "Listernut," and "Listermint." When asked his name by people he met for the first time, he responded with "Velt" to avoid the pejorative comments.

Velt was the first member of the Nelms family to graduate from college, having finished the Black college in Tisdell in 1964 with a degree in English. He had planned to go on to graduate school, but decided to teach for a couple of years first. He got a job at McNeil Consolidated High School, named for the well-liked and long-time Superintendent, Reese McNeil. At the time Velt applied, the Black principal, Samuel Oglesby, had offered a language arts job to a teacher from Tisdell, where he got most of his instructors. The superintendent overrode the Principal's decision and gave the job teaching 9th-grade English to Listervelt who was, in his words, "one of my boys." It was not that Principal Oglesby opposed his former student, but he had already given his word to another applicant. Hiring Listervelt generated no hard feelings on the part of any party involved, except perhaps the other candidate.

Listervelt had been teaching for a few months at McNeil High when he met Paula Anne Tiller, who was at the school looking for the superintendent. Velt thought she was the most stunning woman he had ever seen. She was tall, thin, but not skinny, and with a butt unlike any White woman he had ever seen. Her hair was red, but not real red, as one could see flowing from underneath her wide-brimmed fedora, which looked like a man's hat. She wore a red dress buttoned down the front with a neckline that revealed a soft brown neck; her complexion was quite dark for a White person, and her gold earrings, which looked like miniature chandeliers, hung halfway between her ears and shoulders. Velt surprised himself by noticing so many details about a woman.

As Paula passed Listervelt in the hall, she said hello and smiled slightly. Velt sensed a genuineness that he never felt before in an interaction with a White person. He whiffed the aroma of her perfume and immediately wanted to follow her to the end of the earth. He stood motionless, and she noticed his staring at her like a deer in headlights.

"Are you okay?" she asked.

"I'm fine, forgive me," Velt said.

"Forgive you for what?" she asked.

"For staring at you—you are just so beautiful. I...I'm sorry," he said, realizing that he was talking that way to a White woman, or any woman for that matter.

"Thank you, I think." She started to walk away, but turned around and said, "I'm looking for the English teachers who are meeting today with the superintendent. Do you know where they are?"

"Certainly. I'm going there myself. I'll show you." Velt said, quite surprised that they were going to the same meeting.

When they arrived, the other English teachers, Wanda Basket and Roberta Terrell, and a few instructors from other departments, were waiting along with the principal and superintendent. Mr. McNeil introduced Mrs. Paula Ann Tiller as the new curriculum director for Nelms County. Listervelt was flabbergasted that in some ways she was going to be his "boss" and he had made a fool of himself.

The meeting lasted less than half an hour, as the purpose was for all to get to know one another. The teachers had to introduce themselves and explain how the new director might be of assistance to them. When it became Velt's turn, he managed to make some remarks about more supplies and audiovisual support, even though he thought that he had been completely incoherent. When the meeting ended, Mrs. Tiller said she looked forward to working with them. Listervelt decided he should apologize for saying that she was beautiful, a *faux pas* on two accounts—she was White *and* his curriculum supervisor.

"Mrs. Tiller, I should not have made those comments earlier. I'm sorry," Velt explained.

"Again?" she asked. "Did you mean what you said?"

"Well, ahh, of course, but I should not have said it, and I apologize for saying it," Velt struggled.

"You have not breached any etiquette with me," she said. "I'm glad you said it, if you meant it. Where is that coffee your principal mentioned? Are you going to get a cup?"

"I'm not big on coffee. My Aunt Rena says it will make me black," Velt joked, trying to relieve the tension, but feeling he had put his foot in his mouth again. Paula started to leave to get coffee, thinking that her offer was rejected, but quite confused as to how a cup of coffee could make a Black person black!

"I would love a cup of coffee," Velt said.

The other teachers soon left, and Paula and Velt had a conversation that lasted almost an hour. Velt learned that Paula (she told him to call her that, which he agreed to do only when no one else was around) was born in Virginia but grew up in Kansas. She graduated from a woman's Methodist College in North Carolina, a sister institution to the Black college in Tisdell, and had participated in several conferences that involved Black and White college women. Their views on social issues, though race was not discussed, were almost identical, a coincidence even more amazing than her dark skin and Black butt.

Maybe in another life she was Black, Velt thought.

Paula had come to Nelms County by way of marriage to a man who was now stationed at Fort Washington in Tisdell. Velt gleaned from older teachers that she was the first person in that position who was serious about working with the Black teachers. She talked of getting instructors new equipment, acquiring new textbooks for students, holding integrated meetings of all those under her charge, and working for parity of salaries—ideas that were revolutionary for Nelms County. Paula's liberal thinking surprised Listervelt, who wondered if Superintendent McNeil had any idea of what he had done. The Civil Rights Bill had just passed, but the schools were still segregated and members of the school board had undergone no metamorphosis in their attitudes.

Evidently she doesn't know where she is, Velt thought.

Every month, Paula met with the English teachers and Listervelt could not wait for the meetings so that he could see her again. His attitude unwittingly aroused the suspicions of the other English teachers, who were very generous in giving him individual advice which came in a uniform package: "Stay away from that White woman if you know what's good for you."

Paula and Velt stayed after the others left the meetings. Velt got the impression that Paula's husband was a tightwad (which made him hate him, since he would have given her anything) and somewhat abusive (which made him want to protect her). She said that her husband made her feel insecure and question her ability. This was difficult for Velt to understand, because she was so smart.

Paula and Velt both wanted to earn a doctorate degree some day and it was around this common aspiration much of their conversation revolved. Velt believed Paula was more prepared for that undertaking than he because of her travels and experiences. She had been to France (Paris), England, and Spain as well as most of the states, even Alaska and California. He had hardly left the state of Georgia and had just bought his first car, a white 1961 Ford with a six-cylinder engine. He had never been on a ship or an airplane, only the bus to visit some friends in Georgia, and a train ride up north to visit his cousins in New York. He hung on to her every word, enjoying vicariously so many strange cities and imagining walking the streets of exotic places with Paula hanging onto his arm. Velt began to trust her with the one thing he never entrusted to another human being—his feelings.

One day after the meeting, Paula gave him a small knife with two little blades and an emblem in the handle and said, "whenever you use this knife, you will see my face in this emblem and think of me."

It was common practice in the country for men to carry a little knife, but to Velt this one became special, a symbol of their friendship, an embodiment of their oneness, their essence. Once when the emblem fell off the handle, he thought it was lost. He was so distressed that he treated the loss as if it were Paula herself, like a piece of them had been torn apart. You can imagine the relief he felt when he finally found it.

After about six meetings, Velt decided he had gone long enough without touching this precious specimen of humanity. As they started out the door, he turned to face her and grabbed her hand. Instinctively, she moved closer to him as they stared into each other's eyes. He pressed his lips against hers and opened his mouth to receive the sweetest tongue, as all the stars and galaxies in the universe became perfectly aligned. The kiss grew passionate and Velt unloosed the second button on Paula's dress (the first one she wore open to expose her neck), and then the third button of her dress. All the time their kiss became more passionate, more violent. He unbuttoned the fourth and fifth buttons of her dress and reached around to unhitch her bra to emancipate her perfectly sized breasts. Her nipples hardened and Velt used his fingers to flick them like the toggle switches of a European sports car. His courage unabated, Velt reached to unloose the remaining buttons of Paula's dress, but she pushed his hand away.

"No, no," she said softly but firmly.

Velt was puzzled; he thought she wanted him as much as he wanted her, though the schoolroom was hardly the place to consummate their feelings. Paula pulled herself away and ran into the room where they had coffee earlier.

"I can't do this! I am a married woman. My child, my God, my daughter, I cannot take this chance," she repeated.

Despite saying she was married, Velt noticed only that she did not mention her husband, the inception of what was to become a pattern of selective hearing.

Paula was obviously afraid that she could lose her child in an exposed affair and Listervelt knew as well that they were taking quite a chance. The least of his troubles would be that he could lose his job and embarrass the family.

"Ain't no fool like a Black fool over a White woman," he once heard Aunt Rena say, and *she* used words sparingly.

He recalled the circumstances that prompted the comment. It was years earlier, after the family learned about the lynching of a Black man accused of rape in nearby Converse County. The man was killed even though it was common knowledge in the Black community that the two principals had a long-standing affair. Even worse, a local minister, who had condemned the murder from his pulpit the following Sunday morning and had reminded the congregation that the affair was well known, barely escaped with his own life when the White community learned of his remarks.

At the next meeting, Paula decided that people were noticing that she and Velt were staying later than the others, and she walked out with one of the other women. Velt took her actions to mean that she had ended their relationship. She had given all the teachers some materials to evaluate and he found a note in one of his books. It read:

"Velt, our conversations have been wonderful. I cherish your radiance, wisdom, and tenderness. Call me at my office at 634-5789. We have to be careful."

The next day, he called her. She could not talk, but agreed to meet Velt at his house at 8:00 p. m. if he would give her directions.

Velt lived alone in the home his father left him, and he told Paula to park on the side of the house which was away from the road. She arrived at the time they had agreed on, dressed exactly as she was when they first met. Paula's husband was away for three days and her daughter was being cared for by a neighbor. Velt had never been married, and some relatives were even afraid he might not be straight.

They finished a glass of wine, Velt's favorite merlot, a drink introduced to him by Jewish professors Lewis and Sarah Goldstein, a husband and wife from New York who taught history and philosophy, respectively, at the Black college in Tisdell. The professors invited students over to their house in a White neighborhood where they discussed world affairs, the so called "race problem," learned to play chess, and drank wine. Some neighbors objected to these interracial gatherings and during one session someone threw a brick through the picture window. Velt sometimes drove Junior's car to school and Mrs. Goldstein would see him leaving campus and jump in the car for him to drive her to the store to get cigarettes. One evening Velt was going to a Black bar called the Buick Club where students hung out, and she went with him and made the students there a little nervous.

The students really liked the Goldsteins, the way they flaunted the racial mores and the school rules, serving alcohol to students and discussing issues that school officials thought would cause problems. Dean Richard Morehouse threatened to fire them for disturbing the tranquility of the campus and undermining the morals and ideals the college sought to instill in its students. The Goldsteins responded by posting an essay on the bulletin board in the administration building entitled "This Is Not Heaven." The essay began with a copy of the poem about the courage to change things you can, the patience to accept those you cannot and the wisdom to know the difference, or words to that effect. They then claimed it was the stupidest poem ever written and that most achievements in the world resulted from overturning accepted wisdoms. They argued that college was about taking chances, challenging assumptions, and pushing boundaries—not complacency. Afterwards, the Goldsteins planned another party and sent their students invitations with the heading: "Invited to Disrupt Heaven."

Velt went into the kitchen to get more wine. When he returned, he found Paula nude, standing, waiting for him, and wearing only those chandelier earrings. He put down the glasses and kissed her softly as she unclothed him. He gently pushed her backward toward the large sofa where they had been sitting, until she positioned herself where he could take her. Velt had a fleeting thought of inadequacy, knowing Paula had been around the world and he had so little experience with sex. His inadequacy returned when he finished far more quickly than he wanted to—and she was so good. He just didn't know what she thought of him, but was sure he would not ask. More than anything, he wanted to please Paula. It was still early, and they talked and sipped more merlot. Velt wondered how she could be so good in bed.

"You are wonderful. You have had so much more experience than I have, being married I mean," Velt said.

"I guess you don't need to have experience when you have a partner you care about. You make love as perfectly as anyone could possibly expect." Paula sensed Velt's insecurity.

"You really mean it," Velt said.

"Yes, I do. You are a perfect fit." She said firmly. "Remember when we first met? We don't say what we don't mean, do we?"

They had not really thought about putting on clothes. Velt sat on the sofa and she sat between his legs on the floor as they sipped wine and talked while he played with the nipples of her breasts. Paula felt Velt growing against her back and turned around on her knees and carried him off to a place he had never dreamed about. Velt was momentarily puzzled, elated to have found her "sweet spot" but concerned that people called what she was doing perverted. Yet, it did not seem bad at the time as he appreciatively flicked her earrings before pulling her up to assume a more traditional position.

Velt was now certain that he was completely out of her league. He played in the minors, but she was in the major league.

How can I trust her with my emotions? he wondered. *She has had so many different experiences.*

Finally, Velt succumbed to his insecurity. He asked, "was I really good, Paula?"

"Yes, you are the most magnificent lover I have ever had," Paula reassured him.

Velt was silent even though Paula had paid him the ultimate compliment. Again, he was indulging in selective hearing. His focus was not on "the most magnificent lover" but on the "ever had."

"Is something wrong?" she asked.

"No, no, well, not really; I was wondering how many is 'ever had,' What does that mean?"

"Do you really want an answer to that question?" She certainly had enough experience to know he didn't really want her to be truthful. She also thought the question was totally inappropriate, but decided to indulge him. She cared about Velt's feelings and wanted him to be comfortable with their relationship.

"Yes, I do." Velt was insistent.

Paula thought she would lie but changed her mind. "Six, with you, how is that?" Paula responded.

She explained that Velt was six and her husband was five. She said until now she had been loyal to her husband. Paula started to walk him through the four others. The first was a high school sweetheart whom she had made out with in his car. When she got to number two, Velt had had enough. Number two was a man she had met while working at a non-profit organization while she was in college. He was kind, thoughtful, and completely in love with her. He had been so "enamored," the word she used, that she had made love to him out of compassion.

My God, Velt thought, *what a line, how could she fall for such a bunch of crap?*

"He was in pain, I could tell," Paula anticipated.

Velt was smoldering over what he had heard, and could not drop the subject. He said, "how could you? Were you married?"

She had told him she was not married, but he evidently had forgotten or engaged in selective hearing again. Velt acted as if she were not married at this very moment and in bed with him. Paula became angry – for her honesty, this was the thanks she got. She stood up, grabbed her clothes, and started out the door, dressing as she went along.

"Who the hell are you to judge me?" she shouted. "I'm not promiscuous. Four men before my husband! What was so wrong with that?"

"I'm sorry, I just care so much about you. I wish I could have you all to myself," Velt explained.

She hurried on to the car, with Velt following, dressing and crying without saying anything. Velt sensed that anything else he said would only get him in deeper trouble. He opened her door; she got in and started the car as Velt stood outside pleading for forgiveness. She rolled down the window as she calmed down and used her little finger to beckon him closer. When his head was inside the car she whispered, "you already *had* me... all to yourself."

She stepped on the accelerator and sped away even though Velt had hardly removed his head from inside the window. He wondered if he would ever see her again.

At the next meeting, Paula and Velt did not talk. He called her at the office and she agreed to come by so they could clear the air. She forgave him and they spent more than a year in a secret love affair that no one in the country knew about. They met in places like Atlanta, Columbia, and Charlotte. The relationship satisfied Velt completely even though its clandestine nature convinced some family members that he was gay. In 1966, Paula decided that she would pursue her dream of a Ph.D. and got accepted into a program in psychology at a school in Philadelphia, Pennsylvania. Her husband had already forbidden her to go, and threatened her with divorce, but she decided to go anyway. Paula told Velt of her plans and he encouraged her to follow her dream. He thought that her decision and a divorce would allow them to be together despite the distance, but her husband did not follow through on his threat.

After Paula left, Velt wrote her three or four times a week and her responses came just as often. A few months later, Velt drove to Philadelphia, where he spent two wonderful days with Paula. He even visited a nearby Quaker campus with the thought of trying to get into a doctoral program himself. Of all the White religious groups, Velt admired the Quakers most of all. Velt returned home and continued to write, but Paula's letters became fewer and fewer. He called her about returning to Philadelphia, but was told that that was not a good idea. His letters soon went unanswered, and Paula became more difficult to reach. Velt sent her flowers with a note but received no response.

Finally, about two weeks after sending the flowers he managed to get Paula on the phone. She was polite but matter of fact. The tone, if not the words, told Velt it was over, but he could not accept it. When he mentioned the flowers Paula asked, "were those from you?" He was hurt. He felt like he had been run over by one of Blanton's old busses. "I thought they were from my husband," she said with no mention of the note.

Later, she said she thought they might have been from another student whom she had helped with his work. *She lied.* The only person Velt thought incapable of lying, lied.

Velt was so distressed that he lapsed into depression. He remembered seeing his Uncle Matt pray before going to bed, but rejected the idea. *Besides,* he thought, *isn't it blasphemous to ask God to preserve an adulterous relationship?*

He was mixed up, but he couldn't let go. She had promised him that if they ever decided to part they would make love one last time. She lied about that too. It wasn't Paula he loved, he decided, it was his perception of her that he loved. Yet, he could not let go. She was too much a part of him. He hurt so much for so long he resorted to the one thing that made sense—the bottle.

Listervelt had never confided in anybody about Paula, but he had given Lonnie a letter and told him to open it only if something happened to him. It was his way of responding to Paula's concern that he lived alone. The letter read:

"Lonnie, if you are reading this letter, you know something has happened to me. Please call this number (634-5789) and ask to speak to Paula. Identify yourself only when you are certain no one else hears, and explain to her what's wrong. Thanks."

On the night that he had thrown away Paula's gifts, he had retrieved the letter from Lonnie and tore it into pieces. Lonnie asked about its contents, but Velt did not explain.

Velt came home late tonight, sober, for the first time in three months. He had almost lost his job (showing up late, red-eyed, and unkempt). He entered the house through the kitchen door and went to the refrigerator and got a large glass of orange juice. He sat down at the table and inadvertently glanced into the corner of the room where his single-barrel shotgun, a gift from his father, had gone unnoticed for years. Funny, tonight the gun stuck out like one of the signs that flickered on and off in Uncle Matt's store, which fascinated him as a young boy.

Velt took out the knife Paula had given him and flicked the blades open and shut on his finger, deliberately cutting himself and letting the blood stream down his arm. He wanted to feel pain, physical pain, to match his emotional agony. He reached into the kitchen closet from where he sat and pulled out an old broom that looked like it should have been replaced years ago. He refilled his glass with orange juice and left the carton on the table. He began whittling about ten inches down the broom handle. His mind reflected on the events since he met Paula. What would he do without her in his life?

He hurt so badly that he lost the self-confidence that insulated him from the whispers of alleged homosexuality. He cursed her. He loved her. He hated her. He wanted her. He wrote again and tried to guilty her into coming back to him by repeating the promises she had made to him. He knew now she had another lover – LUCKY SEVEN! He decided to write her a note and tell her how he felt, but he scribbled the letter and threw it on the floor. Again, he tried and discarded the note.

Paula once said that she liked giving him things. He recalled the one gift that he had bought for her; she had asked him to buy something "that you want to take off me." He had purchased a silk negligee and had given it to her just before she left for graduate school, and she had worn it the time he visited her in Philadelphia. One night he took all the gifts that she had given him—a watch, a tie, a shirt, a key chain, a black leather jacket —and threw them in the trash. He had kept the knife, perhaps because he carried one before they met, but more likely because he just could not let go of everything.

"PLOCK." A piece of the broom handle Velt had been whittling on fell to the floor and brought him out of his thoughts. He picked it up, went to the corner of the room, and grabbed the shotgun. For a moment, he thought how much his father had been right for hating White people. Deep down, he knew color meant nothing to Paula, but he had become irrational. She would never have treated a White man this way—the treatment of her White husband was not in his frame of reference. He held the gun between his knees and feet, laid back the hammer, took the piece of broom handle, and stuck it through the trigger with about an equal amount on either side. Paula would know once and for all how much she hurt him. He stuck the barrel of the gun in his mouth, grabbed the piece of handle on either side, and started to mumble, "God forgive—" when a huge, sudden gust of wind threw open the kitchen door and started banging it against the wall – bang – bang - bang. The wind whirled around in a circle, knocked everything off the table, threw the dishes from the cabinets, and pulled the curtains from the windows.

Velt jumped to his feet, only to be caught in a vortex of wind that twirled him around and around as he screamed, "oh my God, oh my God." A minute later, the twisting, whirling wind slithered through the kitchen window and left a great calm. Velt, dazed and half blind, felt his face, his arms, all over his body to see if he were still alive. He picked up his car keys and staggered out the door to his Ford—at least it was reliable, he thought—started the car, and drove off, thinking a "ghost wind," his father perhaps, had saved him.

A couple days later, the family realized Listervelt was missing. They found dishes all over the kitchen, pieces of a broom handle on the floor, a broken shotgun, and the entire room in chaos. Ronnie picked up scraps of blood-stained paper from the floor and theorized that someone named Paula held the key to all of this.

Chapter 14

THE GIFT OF DISCERNMENT

A thing with horns cannot be
completely covered.

African Proverb[11]

*S*ome people in the country thought that education and religion were incompatible. Reverend Whatley was one of
these individuals, but he believed the handicap could be overcome. He made Lonnie his personal project and sent for him,
since he had not seen him since he read the church history. For
his part, Lonnie thought that Rev. Whatley wanted to see him so
he could condemn his "atheistic" ways. The truth is Lonnie grew
up convinced God would punish him for missing religious services and had come to believe that the purpose of that Mourners'
Bench was not to be saved, but to plant a homing device in young
people that brought them back to church as adults.

Lonnie believed firmly in a Benevolent Being and frequently
visited different denominations, from Pentecostal to Unitarian,
seeking spiritual understanding for the complex questions of life.
He knew that enlightenment wasn't to be found at Mt. Canaan,
with all its disorganization. He did enjoy the singing, especially
the hymns raised by the deacons and those impromptu songs
that popped out of any corner of the church. In the old days,
the piano was the only instrument in the church, but recently
guitars, drums, saxophones, and cymbals had invaded the choir
stand. They reminded Lonnie of Miss Chester's House of Prayer
in Tisdell when Bishop Daddy Grace came to town. They also reinforced his belief that Black ministers like Rev. Whatley thought

the greatest scripture in the Bible was "make a joyful noise unto the Lord." Lonnie said he envisioned God about 11:30 a.m. on Sunday morning putting on these giant earmuffs because He knows Black folks are getting ready to go to church.

Despite his reluctance, Lonnie made his way to Mt. Canaan on the third Sunday, as he had done so many times as a young boy. At the end of the program, Reverend H. J. Whatley delivered his sermon in the anti-intellectual fashion Lonnie expected. He concluded as follows.

"Stand up, put your hands together, unless you are too cute or too e-d-u-m-u-c-a-t-e-d," he declared. "Education can't get you into the kingdom of Heaven. Degrees will not get you into the Kingdom Land. You must have a BA—a Born Again—degree. You don't need a Ph. D. but a GOD. I don't know about you, but I would rather arrive in heaven ignorant than to arrive in hell Ph.D. in hand."

The congregation applauded while Lonnie pondered, "why do preachers say that education will not get people into heaven, but fail to explain how ignorance improves their chances."

He thought of Booker T. Washington, who claimed that he was afraid to learn to read because every person he knew who could read or write got the "call" to preach, and he might get one of those calls. Lonnie wondered how this "call" that preachers received endowed so many men with such great ability.

Lonnie had never walked out on a sermon; the closest he had come to leaving was at a funeral for a school teacher named Miss Virginia Sims when the minister said during her eulogy: "Slavery was good, y'all. *Y'all here, ain't you?*"

He thought the remark insulted every ancestor who endured the horrors of this brutal institution. Would a rabbi ever say, "the Holocaust was good, y'all, y'all got Israel didn't you?"

Lonnie's thoughts were abruptly returned to the present by the shouting of someone beset by the Holy Ghost. It was a well-known fact that Whatley preached until someone got "heist-ed." There was even talk among some members that their shout-ing was preplanned. Lonnie already knew that Rev. Whatley had a meeting after the morning service and the program would not last long as usual. "CPT" might mean "Colored People's Time" somewhere, but in the Black church it means "Colored Pastors' Time." In his classroom, Lonnie told students "CPT" stood for "Can't Pass This." After the benediction, Rev. Whatley found Lonnie.

"Lonnie, my boy, what did you think of today's sermon?"

"It was alright," Lonnie said half-heartedly. It had taken Lonnie all the dishonesty he could muster to say that the sermon was okay.

"You approve of my comments, then?" Whatley pushed the issue.

"No, I do not. You need to be advocating education, not knocking it. These people should be told it is God's will to edu-cate their children, that it is a sin not to send their children to school, not to develop their talents to the fullest. What kind of lives are they going to have without an education?" Lonnie said.

"There's all kinds of education, my boy, now let ..." the Reverend was interrupted.

Deacon Diggs had come for Rev. Whatley before Lonnie learned what he wanted. He already knew that Rev. Whatley was holding a conference to deal with a young woman who had be-come pregnant out of wedlock.

Lonnie moved to the back of the church and sat down to ob-serve the proceedings. While he waited, his mind wandered back to his sister Elizabeth, who had told him how she got involved in one of these episodes when the church was expelling another young woman for an unwed pregnancy. Elizabeth was home visit-ing before she moved back for good and Lonnie recalled the story, beginning with her attachment to Rena.

The family was leaving the morning service at Mt. Canaan when Miss Florine Grant said to Rena, "morning, Rena, that your step daughter there?" looking at Elizabeth, the little girl following closely behind Rena.

"Not *STEP*, just daughter," Rena said.

Elizabeth smiled mightily at the remark, "not step, just daughter" which was indelibly stamped upon her mind. When she grew up, Elizabeth explained what this experience meant to her. The "step," like the "but" people used about dark-complexioned people, "pretty, but," was inherently differentiating to Elizabeth.

Elizabeth was very religious even as a child. She adopted Matt's practice of reading the Bible each night and praying at the bedside. She also stood up to Matt when others were afraid, using reasoning and quoting scripture to stand her ground. She also developed some peculiar attachments to animals and even had a pet snake that hung around the well where the family had to get water. She talked to it like it was somebody she knew. Matt said it was just a harmless garden snake, but the only distinction for most Black folk was dead or alive. One day, Trask stumbled on to Elizabeth's "pet" snake and killed it. Elizabeth buried it and refused to speak to Trask for weeks.

It is uncertain whether Elizabeth named her snake, but she had a favorite cow she named Belle, a horse she rode named Booth, and a cute little dog she called Bambo. Matt purchased Belle and Booth, but Elizabeth found Bambo down by the road. She claimed Bambo had class, because he was well-trained before she found him. He could stand on his hind legs, roll over with the twist of an arm, fetch things that you asked him to retrieve, and never begged for food while you were eating. Elizabeth tried to keep him in the house at bedtime, but Rena drew the line here, so she prepared him a bed on the front porch. Everybody believed that Bambo belonged to a wealthy White family until he broke his right front leg and did not fit in with the family anymore since he walked with a limp. Jake said White people were like that. "Retarded" children were put away too, because they couldn't fit in. Black folk, he said, weren't that way.

"Why do you think Combat isn't locked up somewhere?" he asked. One can only guess that Jake failed to remember that the Helgartens' mentally challenged son Louis stayed at home, and he was White.

An incident occurred in the mid-1930s when Elizabeth was about seventeen years old that badly shook her faith. In those days, ministers stayed with members of the congregations where they preached, especially during week-long revivals that lasted way into the night. One Friday after a particularly long revival, Matt invited Reverend Amos Jenkins to be an overnight guest at his house. After the evening meal and a prayer, the family and Rev. Jenkins retired for the night. Elizabeth was assigned the task of cleaning the table and washing the dishes. The minister was given a room by himself, which meant family members had to double up.

After finishing her tasks, Elizabeth was going to her room, a route that brought her past the room assigned to Rev. Jenkins. As she started to pass the door, it opened and Reverend Jenkins stepped out into the darkened hallway. Elizabeth stopped to see what he wanted. In a whisper, he said to her, "lil girl, lil girl, come over here; come on. Come on. I want you to sneak back here tonight."

Elizabeth started to walk away, pretending she didn't hear, but the reverend was insistent on getting her to listen.

"Pssh, pssh. Lil girl, over here," Rev. Jenkins said.

"Yes sir—you want something?" Elizabeth said finally.

"You think you can come back here about 2 o'clock?" he repeated.

"What are you talking about!" Elizabeth said loudly.

"Shh, shh, not so loud. Could you come back later?" the

reverend repeated.

Elizabeth ran to her room, where she spent a sleepless night, unable to shake the ugly image of Rev. Jenkins and his indecent request—standing there in his long white drawers with this white rag on his head knotted at the top, looking like the devil himself. This diabolical image haunted Elizabeth all night, as she pondered what to say to Matt and Rena, especially Matt. By morning, she had decided to say nothing, but she could not bear to look at Rev. Jenkins at breakfast, and pretended to be sick. It was not a school day, so she stayed in her room. Rev. Jenkins was undeterred. Under the pretense of getting something from his room, he left a note under the lamp for Elizabeth before leaving for Tisdell.

"Lil girl you so pretty, the prettiest I ever seen. Hope you will be a good girl until I come visit again."

Later that day, Elizabeth took the note to her grandmother, who destroyed it and promised never to tell Matt. Elizabeth suspected Matt found out anyway, since Rev. Jenkins never again preached at Mt. Canaan. She was hurt though when Grandmother Staten asked if she had done anything to encourage the good preacher, a question that hurt Elizabeth in the asking. The entire incident made Elizabeth question her faith, but she finally concluded that Rev. Jenkins was not a true preacher; he wasn't even a Christian. He was the worst kind of sinner, by pretending to be a man of God. Elizabeth was convinced that he would burn in hell for all eternity.

Elizabeth had been thinking about going north before the incident with Rev. Jenkins. At this time, she would have been the first one to go, but her motive was to make something out of her life so she could help the family. Some people left the South because of racial persecution, but Elizabeth rarely mentioned race. She did say that some southern Christians were Rev. Jenkins-type of Christians and the term "southern hospitality" was an example of their hypocrisy.

"The first word in 'hospitality' is 'hospital'—I guess that's the part meant for Black folk," she said.

In the middle of the nation's worst depression, Elizabeth left Nelms County and moved to Philadelphia, Pennsylvania to live with her aunt Ethel Hester. Matt missed her so much the first year that he drove there to see her. He took eleven-year-old Matt Jr. with him, along with his longtime friend "Uncle" Tommy. He promised to take Hattie, but slipped off from her and took Trask instead. Every night, Hattie sat by the window and cried so that Rena sat down and wrote Matt a letter to tell him to come home, and on that same night they returned. After that, Matt had to earn Hattie's trust.

"Dad would never tell me anything else—like he would always tell me 'no' or 'yes' after that," Hattie said.

Elizabeth got a job as an orderly in a big hospital and began studying to become a practical nurse. After a while, she started sending small amounts of money and care packages home. She also studied under her new pastor and some years later became licensed to preach, eventually becoming an associate minister in her church.

After almost thirty years, Elizabeth returned to Nelms County. She rejoined Mt. Canaan Church and quickly developed a reputation for helping people, but Black ministers didn't tolerate female preachers. She didn't seem to mind that she was never invited to sit in the pulpit. Unlike most Baptists, Elizabeth stuck to a strict diet, fasted, and meditated, which seemed to have made her contented with her faith. She often said, "there is no blueprint way to worship God."

People come to know God ordinarily when they are in trouble or sick, she said, but you should stay close to God all the time. When Trask was sick up in Rochester she went there to take care of him.

"Brother, you need to pray," Elizabeth said.

"I do pray, but I don't wear my religion on my sleeve like you." Trask appreciated her help but not her lecturing.

"You probably pray, but now you are SICK! You can't pray the way you always prayed, 'Now I lay me down to sleep …' You must ask for God's help! You have to pray deeper and stronger, 'Lord, my God, I need you now, I'm sick. Help me,' and MEAN IT. Search the scriptures and see," Elizabeth counseled.

In all honesty, Trask had not thought to pray that way. The same night he picked up a Bible and came across James 5:16 and the words of Elizabeth: "Confess your faults one to another, and pray one for another, that ye may be healed. The effectual fervent prayer of a righteous man availeth much." He also saw in St. Luke 22:39 where Jesus was in the Garden of Gethsemane. "And being in an agony He prayed more earnestly; and His sweat was as it were great drops of blood falling down to the ground."

Trask prayed earnestly for the first time, and the next day he felt better and stronger than any time in the last month. He began to think Elizabeth was the saint people claimed. He remembered that she always believed God had given her a special gift, the gift of clarity. She never claimed clairvoyance, but she said God allowed her to see things clearer than most people. Elizabeth called it "the gift of discernment." One of its basic tenets was that no one was irredeemable. Trask now felt he was the beneficiary of that gift.

On the Sunday Lonnie was remembering these things, Elizabeth had accompanied the family to church and they all sat on the back pew where he was reminiscing, except Matt, who was up front with the deacons. The purpose of the conference that interrupted Rev. Whatley and Lonnie was to decide the fate of fifteen-year-old Diane Alcorn, who had become pregnant without the benefit of marriage. The congregation was to hear from Diane before deciding whether to expel her from the church. The

deacons, including Matt, stood in judgment of this young woman. The deaconesses, the wives of deacons who sat opposite them
in their white dresses, little white hats, and small white veils, had
no voice in the matter. Rena never sat with them and never wore
that white outfit. Perhaps since the deaconesses did not have a say
in any matters, except preparing food or placing flowers or some
such things, Rena saw no need to wear the uniform.

Diane was called up before the church congregation, where
she stood with prominent evidence of her transgression. She ac-
knowledged her mistake, made an earnest plea for forgiveness,
and promised never to do such a thing again. When she finished
talking, her father, trustee Richard Alcorn, asked to speak and
made a statement about his daughter's character. He explained
that Diane was a good person, an obedient child, a faithful member of the church, a good Christian, and not a loose girl. To his
knowledge this was her one mistake and he didn't like it any better than they did, but she was his daughter and he had to support her. He said that he and his wife would raise the child as
their own and if they, as parents, could forgive Diane, the deacons
should do no less. Diane was then asked by Rev. Whatley what
she wanted the church to do. Diane said she loved her church,
the congregation, and pastor, and asked to stay in the church. She
reiterated that she had learned her lesson and had asked God to
forgive her and promised never to repeat her mistake.

After listening to the testimony, the deacons, with the pastor's leadership, decided, on unanimous voice vote, to put her
out of the church—that is, to suspend her from membership for
one year as punishment for her deed. She could come back after
that time and ask to be reinstated. The church members had sat
silently through all of this, and Rev. Whatley began his closing
statement.

"Let this be a lesson to those who would transgress the moral
laws of the church. Such behavior cannot be tolerated ...."

Whatley was suddenly interrupted by a voice from the back of the church.

"*What about the boy?*" the voice said.

"Did I hear somebody who wants to speak back there?" Rev. Whatley asked.

"**_What about the boy_**?" the voice repeated more emphatically.

"Stand up so we can see who is talking back there," the pastor requested, as he squinched his eyes and stood on his toes to see who was speaking.

When he finally recognized who was standing, he could not have been less pleased; it was Elizabeth. Matt recognized her too and kept giving her the look to sit down, the same look that when she was a child would have stopped her in her tracks. Elizabeth had watched what had transpired and could no longer keep quiet. Now standing, Elizabeth said once again, "**What about the boy?**"

Of course, Elizabeth did not object to some form of punishment for the girl, but she was outraged at the double standard, since no mention had been made of the boy.

Reverend Whatley and Elizabeth had gone a few rounds before, and he could not have looked forward to this confrontation. Rena avoided Matt's eyes as he continued to shake his head for Elizabeth to be quiet. Elizabeth was not one to be easily ignored when she made her mind up to say her piece—that was the Matt in her.

Rev. Whatley decided to allow her to speak, but not without pointing out that it was his generosity that made it possible and not her right. He said to the congregation, "Let us open our Bibles to First Corinthians, Chapter 14, verses 34 and 35," he instructed the congregation. "Let us read together: 'Let your women keep silence in the churches: For it is not permitted unto them to speak, but they are to be commanded to be under obedience as also saith the law. And if they will learn anything, let them ask their husbands at home: for it is a shame for women to speak in the church."

Whatley was not yet through. "It says in Timothy 2:11-12 that women have no voice in the church, that women should not usurp authority over the man, but must be in silence. Read it for yourselves. Never let it be said that I am not a fair man—come now, sister." Whatley requested Elizabeth to come with obvious indulgence. He had "proved" she had no right to speak.

Elizabeth composed herself. She had planned to employ a few biblical verses of her own to counter Reverend Whatley's scriptural indictment of women, but she resisted, thinking she must wage one battle at a time. She spoke in a conciliatory tone. "What about the boy? Are you going to remove him from the church as well? Did this child conceive this baby alone? Did God visit her like Mary and make her pregnant? Is this an Immaculate Conception? Does not the father of this unborn child bear equal responsibility? What kind of message are you sending to the young men? Do you want them to think it's okay for them to mess around, but not for the girls? And ONLY MEN! Why are only men sitting in judgment of this young woman? Some of you have illegitimate children of your own. Aren't you being hypocritical? Where does this hypocrisy stop? Let's stop it here! If you put out the girl, do the same for the boy! Bring him up here—you know who he is; make him confess too. Let's do the right thing and send a message to these young bulls that if they strut their stuff, the church holds them just as responsible for their behavior as the girls. Let's be fair and equal in our judgment."

Elizabeth concluded her remarks, "Thank you, Reverend Whatley, for this opportunity to speak, and thank all of you very much for listening to me."

As Elizabeth started back to her seat, one could tell that the women were generally supportive by the smiles on their faces and the nods of their heads, but no other woman spoke up, and there was no applause. Elizabeth knew beforehand that she would have to go this alone, and it didn't bother her one bit.

Some deacons called her remarks blasphemous, especially what she said about God making Diane pregnant. Matt thought that Elizabeth was talking about him when she mentioned out-of-wedlock children, but he was not the only one who fit that description. Several other deacons had illegitimate children, and everybody knew Elizabeth was telling the truth. Still, the deacons and pastor stuck to their guns. Without acknowledging any of Elizabeth's complaints, they adhered to the original vote to remove Diane from the church for a year. They did not even consider throwing the boy out, and he was not even identified, though that was hardly necessary since everybody knew who the father was—none other than Deacon Abe Duncan's grandson, Abe Duncan lll. And at the height of hypocrisy, Deacon Duncan had the audacity to cast a vote to suspend Diane.

When the services ended, the families made their usual greetings and chatter, but today the mood was more subdued than usual. All greeted Elizabeth with polite conversation, and a few women congratulated her for her courage. The usual hour outside for Matt and his family was collapsed into only a few minutes. Matt was too mad to socialize. Soon all of them were in the truck prepared to go home, which was just up the road a piece. Elizabeth was in the cab with Matt and Rena. Matt was so frustrated he couldn't even get the truck started. After a few minutes of painful silence, Matt began.

"Elizabeth, you embarrassed me, embarrassed your mama, embarrassed your sisters and brothers. You embarrassed the whole family."

Rena didn't talk much and certainly not to contradict Matt, but she said firmly, "she ain't embarrassed me!"

Encouraged by Rena's uncharacteristic remark, Elizabeth started to interrupt, but she saw that Matt's silence was not there for her to speak, but for him to garner the words to continue.

"Men and women different. A girl who lays with a boy behind her parents' back will lay with a man behind her husband's back. A man may lay with a woman and get up, brush himself off and still is a man, but for a woman the spots remain forever. It's like that spotted bull in the pasture. He can no more rid himself of those spots than a woman can a bad reputation. Men and women are different – that's the way it always has been, that's the way it is, and that's the way it always will be. A fallen woman cannot remove her spots," Matt concluded.

Elizabeth knew this was all wrong and wondered how she could respect such a man, such a hypocrite with his own illegitimate children. She found herself in one of those "moron" things. She loved her father despite these backward views.

Elizabeth thought that this man loved his children, girls as much as boys, more than any man she knew, those born inside and outside of marriage. He gave them a set of values and he was intelligent, upright, compassionate, and in his own way, honest. She tried to tell herself that she hated his chauvinism but not him, but on this day, her "gift of discernment" failed to provide the superhuman capacity needed to tell the difference.

Chapter 15
THE LAST CHALLENGE

Call the sheriff! Make "doc" move!
He's a PhD; he ain't no real doctor!
I can whip him! Put a hat on my head!

*B*aseball was played on weekends and holidays, but on any day of the week a passerby could attest that he saw a checker game going on under a shade tree in almost any community in the country. When people acquired air conditioners, some of them moved the spotted board inside, but God meant pool checkers to be played outside under a tree with enough foliage to provide shade for players and spectators. Men and women of all ages played checkers, even though the fairer sex rarely engaged in the art of trash- talking that made the game so much fun to watch. Checkers brought the generations together, taught young people about competition, and helped them to handle criticisms and failures. Checkers was a vital institution for socializing children in the country.

Black Americans called the game "pool" or "pool checkers"; some called it "Spanish pool." It was played with 24 pieces (12 for each player) that were called "men," on a board with 64 squares, 32 dark and 32 light. The contest took place on either the dark or light squares with the double corner on each player's right and the single corner of the longest diagonal, called the Mason-Dixon, on the left. The object of the game was to capture all your opponent's men or control (lock or pin) them in such a way that they could not be moved. When neither side could capture or pin the opponent's pieces, the game was said to be a draw, but that decision required mutual consent except in two cases dictated by the rules. First, when an opponent reached a certain number of moves (thirteen in a contest between one king and three kings) and second, when the remaining men returned to the same position more than three times.

In standard or English checkers, or what some people called straight checkers, the game played by most White people, a single piece moved forward one square at a time and could not capture backward. In pool checkers, a single piece moved forward and could capture backwards. In both versions, when a piece reached the opponent's last square it was said to have "kinged" and another piece placed on top of it in a process called crowning ("put a hat on my head," trash-talkers proclaimed) to distinguish it from a single piece. Even then in standard or English checkers, the king moved only one space though it could now capture backwards. In pool, a king could move along a diagonal path and jump anything along the way if there were a vacant square immediately behind the piece being captured so that it could land somewhere along the line. A king behaved somewhat like a bishop in chess, but was more powerful. In all cases, a piece was jumped only once and removed only after jumping was completed. Old players called this regulation the turkey rule, the only explanation for the name being that it was so commonly understood that any turkey ought to know it. Clearly pool checkers was a more complex game than the one played by Whites. Some chess players looked down on checkers, and it is commonplace when talking about some complex situation to say, "this chess, not checkers," but the truth is that the best checkers players could learn chess and beat 90% of them – just saying.

At Matt's store, checkers men were soda caps. When one bought a soft drink (usually a Coke or Pepsi) it was opened by sticking the head of the bottle into the opener (a door) on the side of the drink box and pushing down on the bottle, pulling off the cap, which fell into a container below that served as a reservoir for checkers men. One player turned his drink caps up, and the opposing player turned his caps down. Players generally preferred playing all the time "up" or all the time "down," in which case they declared one side black, which always went first, alternating moves thereafter. Otherwise, the up-caps represented black, which went first, and thereafter players took turns playing caps "up" or "down." What other game, Black folk joked, does a black man get to go first and establish the upper hand?

Matt was one of the best checker players, and few players could beat him. He taught all his children to play, boys and girls alike. The older boys and girls played into the night trying to give each other five straights, which was called a "shutout." If a player won several games but fewer than five and lost a game, the opponent was said to have "gotten down" and the scoring started over again from zero or "nothing, nothing." On a night that Matt wanted to play and there were few customers—and that was often, in a country store—each of his children had to win a game before being allowed to quit. Of course, Matt let them win so they could get to bed at a decent hour.

Some people from different areas of the country played by different rules – regional rules—such as the "huff" rule (or what was called the "blow") in which case a player did not take a jump either by choice or oversight. Accomplished players did not play the huff rule, unless the option of forcing the capture was allowed. They felt that blowing favored inferior players, who developed selective blindness to avoid a sequence of shots. Good players maintained that every move should have a connection to the next move. In other words, they saw moves only in combinations, not as single acts, a visualization called "seeing the bull." The result of any combination was a winning advantage unless a player made a sequence of moves that failed to achieve the desired outcome, in which case his opponent accused him of "seeing a ghost."

Matt prided himself on making shots on amateurs that allowed him to sacrifice a man or two (or even more) to capture three or four of his opponent's pieces or to be crowned. As a crowd-pleaser (and all good checkers players were), he enjoyed it very much when the spectators said "man, did you see that," "hot damn," or "Lord hav' mercy." Boastful talk or "trash" talk was part of the game, and there was little sympathy for a sorry player with a weak ego who sat in front of a good player who talked trash and tried to please the crowd at the same time. If the weak player took too much time to move, his opponent asked someone to "call sheriff Cranford" or "get his mama on the phone" to see if she can get him to move. They had to take their lumps while being called "fish," "turkey," "mullet," "chump," "scrubb," "sucker," and even profane things that made them feel like crawling into a hole and dying. Checkers required a thick skin and the only options were to quit or become a better player.

Although Matt was an audience-pleaser, he knew better than to play for shots on skilled players, which put his men in harm's way in hope his opponent would make a certain move. Placing your men in jeopardy expecting a good player to make a mistake could be sudden death, because they knew the right shots too. Matt prided himself on being able to see four or five moves ahead and going for the bull that led to a win. But the opportunity for combinations was rare, and skilled players manipulated for position, which took more time, but paid great dividends in the end. Many opponents of master players claimed when they lost, that they barely lost, and with one more chance they could win. Unfortunately, the next game was still close, but the result was the same. That was the nature of position play and timing, which separated the best players from the scrubbs. Matt claimed that the first few moves determined the outcome of the game and distinguished the masters from the chumps. Players came from all over to play Nelms County's best players such as I-Clare, Sam B., Tops, Runt, Baldy, Freddie G., D. L., Mullet, T- Boy, Tutt, Big

Cee, Mr. Len, Big L., and Matt. They knew each other's strengths and weaknesses like the backs of their hands, but not one of them could tell you all their opponents' real names.

One summer day in 1961, a rather tall Black man from Tisdell came into Matt's store. Although he would not have gone unnoticed, being from the city and all, his dress exposed his origin if not his intentions. He wore a flashy three-piece suit, a red tie that hung down to his fly, matching red socks, a white handkerchief in his coat pocket, a starched white shirt that looked like it could stand up all by itself, a scarf around his neck, and a feathered fedora atop his head. Noticing a checker game going on, he asked if he could play a game or two of "draughts." They said "yes," of course, since anybody who didn't know what the game was called had no chance of playing well. Still, the man was told he had to wait his turn to get his "ass kicked" like everybody else since they were playing the best two out of three in a contest of "rise and fly." While waiting, the stranger tried to impress other spectators with his knowledge of the game. He claimed that men like Napoleon played checkers and it was popular in Russia, Poland, and other places, but none of this impressed his listeners who had no idea where these places were. He even spouted on about how Africans in Egypt played checkers hundreds of years ago, though most thought he was wrong about that too since everybody knew Egypt was in the Middle East.

Soon the stranger got his turn to play and asked players to agree to a few rules. "I play mandatory jumping, no flying king, and any man touched must be moved," he said.

They weren't sure what "mandatory" meant, but they knew what *he* meant so the games began. It did not take the stranger long to dispense with all the chumps in the store, and he was soon surrounded by all the customers who had turned to watch the games. The people learned that he was actually from Tisdell, but he claimed that he had played the best pool players from Auburn

Avenue in Atlanta to Harlem, New York. While the stranger was beating the turkeys, one of Nelms County's best players came into the store and watched. Great excitement was now anticipated with the arrival of "Tops," and the conclusion that this stranger was no scrubb even if he didn't know the game was called "pool" and not "draughts."

When Tops sat down to play the stranger, all gathered around to watch this city boy get what they now knew he justly deserved—a major ass-whopping and a dose of country humility. Tops drew several games, but the stranger beat him two out of three rather easily. So far, the stranger had not even lost a game. He then challenged Matt to a contest, since they all said he was the best. Matt wanted to accommodate him, but it was almost closing time, and Matt joked that he liked to take his time when he put city slickers in their proper place, as they all laughed. Everyone knew by now that this stranger was no ordinary shade-tree player. He was looking to bet money on the game and offered to make a wager. Matt had long since given up gambling so that proposition was, as Rena always said, "barking up the wrong tree." Matt's friends accepted the challenge, however, and decided to put up $100 for the game the next day at a prearranged time.

At promptly 6:00 p.m. the next day, the stranger and two sidekicks returned to Matt's store where the board was already set up. This time he introduced himself to the locals as Billy "Pool" Preston and said boastfully that they might have heard of him.

"Fraid not," Johnnie said "Ain't nobody here done heard of you, and after tonight, dem that done heard of you liable to fergit you."

They all laughed, except the rough-looking couple who came in with Pool Preston —of course, all fly-dressing city fellows looked like toughs to people in the country.

The bet was for $100, and $200 was placed on the counter in an envelope—a lot of money for the time. The winner was the player who won the best three out of five games instead of the usual best two of three. After agreeing on the rules, a coin was tossed to see who would start with the black men and go first. Preston won the toss, but declared as a gentleman he would allow Matt to have black—a concession Matt declined, citing the same reason. Pool Preston then snapped his fingers and one of his comrades produced a bag with large checker men that seemed to be made from marble or ivory.

"I hope you don't mind a better set of men," Preston said.

The audience had seen pool sharks—billiards, that is—come into Kalem's place with their own cue stick, but this was the first time they had seen someone carrying his own set of checker tops.

Matt and Pool Preston played several games, which were longer and quieter than an ordinary checker game as they studied the board and felt each other out. There was no set time to move. The first three games resulted in draws. Matt broke the ice with a win, to the cheers of what must have seemed like the entire Black male population of Nelms County and to the intense stares of the two friends that came in with Pool Preston. Billy Pool tightened up his game, and after a couple more draws took the next two wins to the great pleasure of his two buddies and to the chagrin and disbelief of Matt's supporters. All Preston needed now was one more win to take the match and Matt's friends' hard-earned cash.

Unfortunately, the next game resulted in a major controversy. Matt had one man left, which had been crowned in Preston's double corner section. Pool Preston had three men left, one king on the Mason Dixon, the longest diagonal line that ran from the left single corner to the right single corner of the board, and two single men. Matt asked that the game be declared a draw which was normally done when one opponent has a king and the other only has three men, even though all three may be crowned. He asked Pool Preston to "ring up," the expression used for ending the game to start another. Preston vehemently objected and claimed that the game was a draw only if Matt's single king controlled the Mason Dixon, which it did not. Matt said that this was the way they always played, and the practice was too universal to be considered a regional rule, that's why it was not covered when they went over the rules before the game.

"Besides," Matt said, "you cannot win anyway, Mr. Pool, even when you get three kings. I can tell you sure as God's from Zion."

The children thought Matt was saying "sure as God's from Zion" to express his certainty of some occurrence, but many years later they realized he was saying "as sure as gun's iron."

"I *can* win, Mr. Matt, because I control the Mason-Dixon line. I can win with what we call the special—maybe y'all ain't heard of this down here in this neck of the woods. You can begin counting when I get a third king, and if you count to thirteen, it is *then* declared a draw," Pool explained," but I assure you, you will not get to that magic number."

"Don't let him change the rules, Matt—this must be some 'drafts' rule. This here is pool," Matt's friends declared.

Matt's backers were anxious over their $100. With the score two games to one, and Pool Preston claiming he could win the decisive third game, his friends' confidence was eroding. And few of them could really afford to lose that much money.

"No city slicker can't come in here and change the way we play, Matt," another said. "Ring the game up and start another—he can play 'draft' with somebody else."

"It's okay, boys. You know I don't gamble, but this is worth seeing. If he wins, I'll give you your money back. Let's play, Mr. Preston!" Matt said.

Matt and Preston moved until Pool Preston got his third king crowned in one of the double corners. Another of his kings already controlled the main highway or Mason-Dixon. Matt's king occupied the other double corner and he began counting on his next move—"One." Billy Pool then manipulated his kings to the middle of the board and forced Matt from the double lines. "Four," Matt counted. Preston now controlled the middle of the board as well as the double lines, with Matt carefully avoiding bird traps (a term used for getting caught with a simple shot). "Six," Matt said. Preston's kings formed a triangle and forced Matt's king to one of the single corners. "Eight," he counted. Pool Preston sacrificed one of his kings, ("Nine") and captured Matt's king on the tenth move. The contest was over, with Pool Preston winning three games to one. The crowd appreciated the quality of the play, but was sorry Matt had lost. The two tough guys with Billy Pool now enjoyed themselves heartily.

Matt took five twenty-dollar bills from the cash register and gave them to his friends. He then handed Pool Preston the envelope from the counter which contained two one-hundred-dollar bills. Matt had learned a good lesson and paid a high price for it, but to him it was another example of his philosophy, "an even swap ain't no swindle."

Pool Preston responded, "Mr. Matt, you are a true gentleman. I cannot leave your fine premises without spending some of this money in your store. I have not had sardines and saltines for some time."

He bought sodas and food for all, probably spending almost twenty dollars, a lot of money when a can of sardines, saltines, and drink cost less than fifty cents. After eating his food, Preston returned to the checker board to demonstrate the "special" and some other moves he thought were unknown in the country. The contest became a major item of conversation for years to come.

Life was like checkers to Matt. You win some and you lose some, but you must never lose twice for the same reason. The "special" became a vital weapon in his checkers arsenal, but the confrontation with Billy "Pool" Preston was his last real challenge on the spotted board.

Chapter 16
THE CALL TO THE WATER

In the end the swimmer will be called
by the water.

African Proverb[12]

*I*t was December 6, 1962 that Matt Nelms Sr. passed from labor to reward. The celebration of his birthday the day before had been a happy time as he was surrounded by the four children still in the nest and those who had come home bearing gifts to wish him a happy birthday. Their father showed no signs of a man in his last hours of life. It was a cruel irony that the joy of that day served only to heighten the shock of his passing. To some it seemed a contradiction to a life with many contradictions; a birthday, a time of renewal; and death, a time for closure.

The events surrounding Matt's death began about 4:30 a.m. that December morning with his waking up and calling for Ronnie. Rena rushed out of bed to get him.

"Wake up, wake up boy, wake up. Your daddy want you." Rena shook Ronnie hard and fast.

"What?" Ronnie responded, half awake.

"Wake up. Your daddy sick, he want you in there," she said.

"What wrong with Daddy," Ronnie said as he hurried to his father's bedside.

"What daddy, what daddy, you alright daddy?" Ronnie said with tears in his eyes.

"G-o-o git Kalem," Matt said weakly. "I want to see him."

Ronnie ran into the room to get his pants. "What's going on?" Lonnie asked.

"Mama say Daddy dying," Ronnie responded as Lonnie jumped out of bed. He got his pants and headed out of the house crying, putting his clothes on at the same time as he headed across the road to get Kalem. A few minutes later, Ronnie returned.

"He coming, Daddy—are you alright, Daddy?"

Kalem came in a hurry and went into the room where everybody was now gathered.

"Matt, you want me?" He didn't call Matt "Daddy." He called him "Matt."

"Kalem, I w-a-n-t y-o-u to join the church. You must save your soul, Kalem, you hear me?" Matt said.

"What, Matt? What you want? I can't hear you," Kalem said.

Everybody else heard just fine, though Matt's voice was weak, but Kalem was struggling for time for an appropriate response to a man on his death bed.

"I want you to j-o-i-n the c-h-u-r-c-h." Matt mustered all the strength left in his body to be clear.

"I hear you, Matt," Kalem said without agreeing to join the church.

"Prroommisse me, Kalem," Matt insisted as firmly as his weakened condition would allow.

"You don't know what you are asking," said Kalem, not wishing to lie to Matt on his death bed.

"P-r-o-m-i-s-e m-e," Matt said.

"Okay Matt, I'll try." Matt took this as an agreement because he knew Kalem's word was his bond. Matt had been holding on and died almost immediately with his son's "okay," but not "I'll try," in his ears. Rena's sadness was immediately evident. She must have thought not only of Matt's death but the burden of responsibility which she must now exercise with four teenage children still in the house.

The children didn't know how deeply they loved their daddy until the day he died. Theresa shared her thoughts.

"When someone called on a Sunday morning and said Daddy was dead, it was like a dagger in my chest. I carried that weight around for months. Our relationship with Dad was special. We could tell him anything. He was very loving and easy to get along with. There were four of us girls right together – he called us his 'stairsteps.' We never felt any jealousy with Dad. I felt equally loved, as much as any of the other girls."

The funeral was held a week later. At the service the music was solemn, and all was subdued inside the crowded sanctuary where people lined all around the walls. Outside, where there were twice as many people, the mood was festive, as people greeted one another, chatted and talked, probably exaggerating their times with Matt. Matt's favorite scripture the 23rd Psalm had been read twice, and two of his favorite hymns, "I was a Wandering Sheep" and "Amazing Grace" had been sung. Deacon Dwight Williams had prayed for more than ten minutes, spending more time invoking God's blessings upon all his creatures everywhere than trying to console the family.

Testimonies followed, with the usual superlatives and exaggerations that one scholar calls "testilying." All that was left was the eulogy, and Rev. Whatley, Matt's friend and pastor for almost thirty years arose to speak.

"Brothers and sisters," he began, "we're gathered here today to witness the life and times of our brother Matt Nelms Sr." He noted visitors from all over before continuing. "Today, it is not a day for crying but a day of rejoicing. We can do Matt no good, and we can do him no harm. He labored in the vineyard a long time, and now he gone to receive his reward. Matt already preached his funeral a long time ago—he preached it in the way he ran his business, he preached it in the way he cared for his family, he preached it in the way he loved his neighbors, and he preached it by sitting in that pew [pointing to the deacons' corner]. He lived a life for the Lord. He left a blueprint to follow.

"Live like Matt, and your lives will be alright. A church man, a family man, a deacon, a role model, a pillar of the community. He was a leader and a doer. Look at the different faces gathered here, White and Colored from all over this region." Rev. Whatley paused. "A blueprint for all to follow. He left a plan for his family to follow. A blueprint in the church to follow. He was a Christian model who loved his Lord, his church, his pastor. Take note of YOUR shortcomings, your inability, your unwillingness to live a life like Matt Nelms."

Whatley continued, "Matt Nelms is no longer on this side of Jordan, but who can forget his prayer of forgiveness because 'the things you tell us to do we leave undone, but the things you tell us not to do we rush into like horses in battlefield.' What a marvelous life and a marvelous death! A death in the comfort of home, a death certain of everlasting life. A death without fear – fear only for loved ones not yet in the bosom of Jesus. Will you see him in heaven? Will you get YOUR house in order? Will YOU be saved?" Rev. Whatley was coming to conclusion.

Lonnie always thought Whatley's remarks were aimed at him, but now he knew Whatley was talking to Kalem, whom Matt had tried to convince to join the church. Matt and Kalem had a symbiotic relationship, living next door and working with each other, depending on one another. They had had an earlier bout over this religion thing, which had come to a head when Kalem's daughter, called Lil Liz, wanted to join Mt. Canaan. She slipped off to become a member, and Matt felt proud of her courage to stand up for her beliefs. Kalem himself made a genuine effort to join Mt. Canaan to keep his word to Matt, but he never quite made it. He did try as he promised. Perhaps his Native American heritage continued to militate against organized religion, or he failed to overcome the hypocrisy of churchgoers, particularly since the "church" never stopped coming to him. Eventually however, his wife and all his children became members of Mt. Canaan, even becoming deacons and trustees.

The funeral was attended by many unfamiliar people, but there was one woman who was a real mystery. She entered the sanctuary wearing a black dress that flowed almost to her ankles, but with splits in the sides, a white shawl around her shoulders, and a pair of black boots. She had on a wide-brimmed white hat with a thin white veil that covered her entire face. According to those with the best view, she was in her late forties or perhaps a little older, and very light-complexioned, perhaps even White.

Except for three things, she probably would have gone unnoticed in such a large crowd of mourners. First, her late arrival and the number of fine "gentlemen" who offered her a seat while other women stood along the wall; second, everyone remembered her constantly weeping through the entire service, though she was not alone in that regard. It was the third thing that got everybody's attention. After the eulogy, the coffin was reopened for final viewing of the body before interment. Members of the congregation slowly filed pass the coffin with an occasional individual stopping, some for too long. When this woman made her way to the front of the church, she stopped in front of the coffin, pulled her veil back in a way that would have revealed her face to those in the pulpit except for the flowers surrounding the coffin, and leaned down and kissed Matt right on his mouth. It was shocking enough that this woman would kiss a dead man on the mouth, but some thought the kiss lingered far too long to be decent. Rena paid little attention, perhaps too traumatized to realize what others were thinking. The woman slowly replaced her veil and moved on, still weeping, to the back of the church. When she reached her seat, she pulled her shawl from around the chair and walked outside to leave without waiting for the burial. Many people outside noticed her walk down to the end of the road where she had parked her car, a small black, sleek sports car, a Jaguar, according to Dexter Hawes, who said he had seen one in a book. The woman climbed into her car and left with the engine roaring.

To this day the woman remains a mystery, but theories abound: First among them is that the mystery woman was Matt's daughter. Second is that she was a relative, perhaps a sister on his father's side who had crossed the color line. These theories many dismissed since the old people did not know her. Third and most prominent was that she was a lover with whom Matt had maintained a romantic relationship. This theory persisted because it fed the rumor mill in ways that other theories did not.

Reverend Whatley saw in Matt's death another of his now-famous metaphors with the spotted bull and the fence. He told the congregation that Matt's death was a symbolic leap of the bull over all obstacles. That his death was a victory and his happiness the previous day was no mere irony, but a triumphant preparation for eternal joy.

"If you blueprinted Matt's life, devotion to family, love of church, support for friends and community, for yourselves, the world would be a better place. In death, the bull always leaps the fence, and when you are called to the water, you too will leap from the pasture of this life into the boundless glory of eternal life."

Things got a little rough for Rena and for the four young children after Matt's death. The grown children at home and away could be depended on for financial assistance, but it was Kalem who became more like a father, especially to the boys. Some older children insisted that thousands of dollars owed to Matt by neighbors and others be given to debt collectors, but Rena refused. She said that Matt would never send a White man after a Black man, and she would not do in death what he wouldn't do in life. Many neighbors paid their bills anyway. As time passed, Rena sold the pulp-wood trucks and equipment, some of the land, and the grocery store to Hattie and her husband, but no matter how bad things got, she insisted on keeping "something to leave the children."

ENDNOTES

1. Steven Watson, *The Harlem Renaissance: Hub of African American Culture, 1920-1930* (New York: Pantheon Books, 1995), p. 14.

2. Arnold Adoff, *The Poetry of Black America: Anthology of the 20th Century* (New York: Harper and Row Publishers, 1973), p.71. Quote was taken from Hughes' poem *Cross*.

3. Jan Knappert, *The A-Z of African Proverbs* (London: Karnak House Publishing, 1989), p. 24.

4. Watson, p. 69. Quote is from "How It Feels To Be Colored Me" by Zora Neale Hurston.

5. Carter G. Woodson, *The Mis-Education of the Negro* (Philadelphia: Hakim's Publications, 1933), p.196.

6. Knappert p. 87.

7. Donald Grant, *The Way it was in the South: The Experience in Georgia* (Athens: University of Georgia Press, 1993), p. 351

8. Adoff, p. 22. Quote was taken from poem *Common Dust* by Georgia Douglas Johnson.

9. Woodson, p. 52.

10. Knappert, p. 82.

11. Knappert, p.109.

12. Knappert, p. 31.